"THEY'RE KILLING THE HORSES!"

A hundred yards up the canyon the Lazy K horses were reeling in confusion and panic. They were kicking up enough dust to obscure some of what was happening, but Boyd and Slocum could see at least two horses down and kicking. They could also hear the animals' screams of fright and agony.

Slocum glanced over his shoulder and saw more horses down amid the billowing clouds of dust. He also saw little spouts of dust coming toward them down the arroyo and knew that some of the shooters on the ridge were trying to get their range. Then he felt a solid, thudding vibration through the skirt of his saddle.

"God damn it to hell," Slocum muttered hopelessly.

His pony shuddered and stumbled, pitching itself right into Boyd's path . . .

OTHER BOOKS BY JAKE LOGAN

RIDE, SLOCUM, RIDE
HANGING JUSTICE
SLOCUM AND THE WIDOW
    KATE
ACROSS THE RIO GRANDE
THE COMANCHE'S WOMAN
SLOCUM'S GOLD
BLOODY TRAIL TO TEXAS
NORTH TO DAKOTA
SLOCUM'S WOMAN
WHITE HELL
RIDE FOR REVENGE
OUTLAW BLOOD
MONTANA SHOWDOWN
SEE TEXAS AND DIE
IRON MUSTANG
SHOTGUNS FROM HELL
SLOCUM'S BLOOD
SLOCUM'S FIRE
SLOCUM'S REVENGE
SLOCUM'S HELL
SLOCUM'S GRAVE
DEAD MAN'S HAND
FIGHTING VENGEANCE
SLOCUM'S SLAUGHTER
ROUGHRIDER
SLOCUM'S RAGE
HELLFIRE
SLOCUM'S CODE
SLOCUM'S FLAG
SLOCUM'S RAID
SLOCUM'S RUN
BLAZING GUNS
SLOCUM'S GAMBLE
SLOCUM'S DEBT
SLOCUM AND THE MAD MAJOR
THE NECKTIE PARTY
THE CANYON BUNCH
SWAMP FOXES
LAW COMES TO COLD RAIN
SLOCUM'S DRIVE
JACKSON HOLE TROUBLE
SILVER CITY SHOOTOUT

SLOCUM AND THE LAW
APACHE SUNRISE
SLOCUM'S JUSTICE
NEBRASKA BURNOUT
SLOCUM AND THE CATTLE
    QUEEN
SLOCUM'S WOMEN
SLOCUM'S COMMAND
SLOCUM GETS EVEN
SLOCUM AND THE LOST DUTCHMAN
    MINE
HIGH COUNTRY HOLDUP
GUNS OF SOUTH PASS
SLOCUM AND THE HATCHET
    MEN
BANDIT GOLD
SOUTH OF THE BORDER
DALLAS MADAM
TEXAS SHOWDOWN
SLOCUM IN DEADWOOD
SLOCUM'S WINNING HAND
SLOCUM AND THE GUN RUNNERS
SLOCUM'S PRIDE
SLOCUM'S CRIME
THE NEVADA SWINDLE
SLOCUM'S GOOD DEED
SLOCUM'S STAMPEDE
GUNPLAY AT HOBBS' HOLE
THE JOURNEY OF DEATH
SLOCUM AND THE AVENGING GUN
SLOCUM RIDES ALONE
THE SUNSHINE BASIN WAR
VIGILANTE JUSTICE
JAILBREAK MOON
SIX-GUN BRIDE
MESCALERO DAWN
DENVER GOLD
SLOCUM ON THE BOZEMAN TRAIL
SLOCUM AND THE HORSE THIEVES
SLOCUM AND THE NOOSE OF HELL
CHEYENNE BLOODBATH
THE BLACKMAIL EXPRESS

JAKE LOGAN

SLOCUM AND
THE SILVER RANCH FIGHT

BERKLEY BOOKS, NEW YORK

SLOCUM AND THE SILVER RANCH FIGHT

A Berkley Book / published by arrangement with
the author

PRINTING HISTORY
Berkley edition / August 1986

ISBN: 0-425-09111-2

A BERKLEY BOOK® TM 757,375

Berkley Books are published by The Berkley Publishing Group,
200 Madison Avenue, New York, NY 10016.
The name "BERKLEY" and the stylized "B" with design are trademarks
belonging to Berkley Publishing Corporation.

PRINTED IN THE UNITED STATES OF AMERICA

1

The road led down into a shallow wash and angled up the other side, little more than a slice out of the tan, sun-baked earth where the sage and rabbit brush and greasewood had been cleared away. But when Slocum topped the second rise he was impressed by the layout that appeared below him. Whoever owned the ranch Slocum was crossing had owned it for a long time and had made it into something to be proud of. The narrow windows in the walls of the solid, well-kept adobe house would have been rifle ports in the days of Apache raiding parties. Now the only activity Slocum could see from the ridge was the placid movement of several cows scuffing up a little dust in the corrals by the low-slung barn. The rest of the compound was empty. Nothing else moved around the house or the three tin-covered outbuildings Slocum assumed were equipment sheds. The buildings might have been deserted except for the large garden with its dark parallel stains of recent irrigation.

Things began to look better as Slocum moved closer. He noticed chickens wandering in the yard, sharp white specks in the glare of the sun, and a moment later he could hear a steady clanking from the windmill that was spinning smoothly in a light breeze. Slocum was so pleased with what he saw that he made the mistake of smiling. He stopped in the next instant when he felt his dry lips begin to crack. He touched his mouth, looked at the blood on his fingers, then twisted in the saddle to lay his hand gently on the small calf tied behind him on the horse's rump. The calf kicked once when it was touched, remembered it was hopeless, and settled down again.

"No need to fret now," Slocum said aloud, speaking as a man will after a string of solitary days on the trail. "Your troubles are almost over, and so are mine."

Slocum still didn't let himself smile, but there was a bright sparkle in his eyes under the brim of his hat that had nothing to do with the sun almost straight up above. He was letting his imagination wander in the same direction it had been going ever since he found the calf.

"Fresh eggs and cool well water," he told the calf. "That much I can see already. I think I can even taste 'em." He began to imagine a dinner table covered with great chunks of cooked beef—barbecued, maybe—with hot loaves of fresh bread to sop up the gravy. He imagined slabs of cheese, and a generous crock of butter for the bread. Those had to be milk cows in the corrals, and the presence of a garden seemed to promise that there would be a woman on the ranch who could turn the milk into cheese and butter. He figured that the woman—maybe even women—would stumble all over herself trying to take care of him as soon as she saw the calf he'd rescued.

Slocum turned off the trail just beyond the corrals and walked his little spotted pony up toward the 'dobe, allowing himself a dry chuckle without moving his lips. "Yes, sir," he murmured to the calf, "they'll take one look at those big brown eyes of yours and the women'll go all soft and teary-eyed. They won't be able to do enough. Just think of the cool shade in that barn, and all the soft hay to sleep on. That is, when you're not busy sucking on a new mama with plenty of sweet milk." The gleam in Slocum's eye turned sharper. "But a good feed's the next best thing," he said aloud, "and that's exactly what I got comin', thanks to you. They'll just naturally want to show me their gratitude."

Slocum tried to imagine the rancher's wife. She would be leathery and work-hardened, but he could see her scuttling around the kitchen, preparing the feast he'd already prepared in his imagination.

Maybe the rancher and his wife had a daughter. She would be lonely out here, longing for the hard embrace of a man's arms. The thought sent a little shiver through Slocum's body, the result of too many weeks without a woman. Then his eyes clouded over. Tough old ranchers tended to be pretty careful when saddle bums started hanging around their daughters, and Slocum tended to be pretty careful around tough old ranchers who had managed to survive the Apaches.

Slocum's frown disappeared in the next moment, replaced by the earlier sparkle in his eyes. He decided the old rancher would have a housekeeper. She would be a hot-blooded Mexican or maybe a Pueblo Indian. She'd also be just as lonely as the rancher's daughter would have been, and the rancher wouldn't much care what she did with her time off.

The woman who stepped out of the 'dobe with a Winchester in her hands was neither Mexican nor Indian. She had a full mane of wild red hair and a pale, smooth face with the kind of downturned mouth Slocum could never get enough of. She looked to be a little past thirty. She was staying near the door, in the deep shade of the ramada. Slocum frowned at the carbine she was carrying and saw that the hammer was already on cock. He was staring at the soft lines of her mouth again when the woman demanded, "What do you want?"

Slocum carefully tipped his hat and made a show of resting both hands on the pommel of his saddle. "Excuse the intrusion," he said. "I was just bringing this calf that I found."

The woman came forward a few steps. Slocum noticed how much ground she was able to cover. He realized that she was close to six feet tall and a lot of that was legs, long, lean legs wrapped tightly in a pair of jeans. Slocum felt a sudden weakness that didn't have anything to do with his hunger for food. He tried to meet the woman's steady gaze until she glanced at the part of the calf she could see behind Slocum's hips.

"Orphan?" she asked.

"No sign of a cow within at least a mile," Slocum said with a shrug. "And I looked."

"Why?"

"Ma'am?" said Slocum. She hadn't given the calf more than that one brief look. In fact, none of this was going as he had expected.

"Why did you go to all that trouble?" the woman asked.

"Just to be neighborly, I suppose."

She came forward a few more steps, out from under the ramada, and her hair seemed to catch fire in the sun as she tilted her head slightly to study Slocum's face. Her dark brown eyes were very large and very deep, giving Slocum the impression that nothing would escape them. He watched her gaze drift down again to take in his clothing, the rigging on his horse, the Colt in his holster, and his own Winchester hanging beneath his right leg.

Slocum grinned despite the pain in his lips and said, "I suppose I was also hoping to get a good meal or two. Maybe even a bed to sleep in."

The woman nodded as if satisfied and eased the hammer down on her Winchester, cradling the weapon in the crook of her arm against her body. It pushed her loose cotton shirt against her rib cage, giving Slocum a hard time as he tried not to stare at the woman's breasts swelling out above her rifle. He found it hard to believe that she didn't know what effect she was having on him, but when he studied her eyes he could find no hint of awareness, no look of mocking triumph. She only returned his stare, observing him with a cool and distant expression.

"That's a beautiful set of conchos," the woman said suddenly. "Are they really silver?"

"Yes," said Slocum, once again surprised. "Thank you."

"From Mexico?"

"That's right." Slocum took off his hat because he couldn't think of anything better to do. He looked at the band of silver ornaments circling its crown, then held the hat out to the woman. "Want to take a look?"

She took the hat, but glanced only briefly at the conchos. "These must have cost a lot of money," she said, watching Slocum.

"I'm sure they did," Slocum said with a casual shrug. "I'm sure the man who lost them was sad to see them go." He saw her dark look of suspicion and added, "He lost them in a poker game, unfortunately, and his luck never did get any better."

"You were the lucky one, then?"

Slocum offered a modest grin. "It happens now and then."

The woman returned Slocum's hat. While he was adjusting it on his head she said, "I suppose no one ever tried to take those conchos away from you."

Slocum stared at her for a moment, still off balance. "Of course they tried," he said.

"That's what I thought. And yet here you are."

"A little more luck, I suppose."

"Sure." The woman looked at him a moment longer, a gleam of something like amusement in her eyes. "Well, I'll tell you what," she finally said. "You and your silver conchos are guests of the Rancho de Plata—"

Slocum laughed.

"You understand, then?"

"Sure. Rancho de Plata . . . the Silver Ranch."

"Also called the Lazy K, which is our brand. My father's brand. My name's Rachel Anderson, and we do appreciate your bringing in the calf."

Slocum touched his hatbrim again and stepped off his horse, groaning inwardly. He'd been hoping that she would not turn out to be the rancher's daughter.

"Pleased to meet you," he drawled. "I'm John Slocum, and I sure could use a drink of water."

The woman lifted her chin slightly and pointed it toward the windmill, then waited for him to lead the way with his horse. Slocum noticed that she glanced at the ground for a moment, apparently thoughtful, before falling in by his side with an easy, graceful, hip-swaying stride. "Where'd you find the calf?" she asked.

"South of here, probably five or six miles. Not too far off the trail."

Rachel Anderson looked over her shoulder to the south as she walked, and then, for no reason Slocum could understand, stared off to the north. "You say you were only hoping for a meal and a bed?" she said thoughtfully.

Slocum nodded.

"I'll tell you what, Mr. Slocum. You can have your meal and bed. And some peach pie I've got in the oven right now. And . . . two dollars? If you'll just take me back and show me where you found that calf."

Slocum frowned, stopping in front of a large tank at the base of the windmill. It was built of heavy boards, dark with age and covered in places by thick green moss. The inside was lined with tin, which shimmered through three or four feet of water. A pipe leading from the base of the windmill, resting on the edge of the tank, flowed with a crystal-clear stream of water as the blades turned above with their steady beat. Slocum eyed the water but he didn't drink right away. He dropped his reins and watched his pony dip its head toward the tank.

"I told you straight, ma'am," he said. "That critter was all alone. Not a cow in sight."

"I'm sure you know they return to the last place they've nursed."

"Sometimes, but—"

"I just want to make sure there's nothing we can do for the mother."

"But the calf couldn't have gone that far away. I'm trying to say you'd just be wasting a trip, ma'am. I promise you, I looked real carefully."

"I see," she snapped. "And, naturally, I couldn't be expected to know what I'm talking about. Is that it?"

Slocum was baffled by the bitterness of her tone and the hard look in her eyes. "I don't mean that at all," he said. "I was just trying to be helpful."

"I'm sure you have a good point," said the woman, suddenly contrite, "but I would still like to go. Don't forget that whether it turns out to be a waste of my time or not, you'll still have an extra day's pay in your pocket."

"It's your money, Miss Anderson."

The woman gave him a brilliant smile. "Exactly! Besides, did you have any better plans today than going for a ride with me?"

Slocum laughed, then winced with pain. He touched his fingers to his lips and once again looked at the fresh blood on them.

"We have something in the house for those lips," the woman said. "I'll go get it while you drink your fill. And I'll take the pies out of the oven. Would you mind putting the calf into an empty stall in the barn?"

Slocum said he would do it, then watched the woman walk back toward the house before he bent over the water pipe. He kept the image of those long legs in his mind as he cupped his hands beneath the stream of water and drank, feeling the cold water hit his belly. He thought it was a shame that such a woman should be hidden away on a ranch in the middle of New Mexico. He also tried to imagine what she hoped to accomplish by retracing his steps. He was fairly sure it wasn't just a matter of finding the calf's mother. She seemed too tense, too thoughtful, as if her dark eyes were hiding some deeper workings of her mind.

He was even more sure of his hunches when she reappeared in the yard, still carrying the Winchester, and now wearing a holstered revolver as well.

2

"Do most people fall for it?" said Rachel Anderson.

Slocum straightened up in the saddle, staring at her. It was the first time she had spoken to him in almost an hour. "I never know what you're gonna come up with next," Slocum said with a laugh. "And half the time I don't even know what you're talking about when you do say it."

"Don't you really?"

Slocum turned in the saddle as he rode, to get a closer look at the woman. There was the faint twist of a smile on her lips, which matched his own.

"Now see," she said, "you're forgetting your game. If you were just another cowhand riding the grubline, you'd be all embarrassed and fiddling with your hands. You wouldn't be sitting there trying to figure me out."

Slocum laughed again. "I guess you have a point," he said. "But if you were like most ranch girls I wouldn't have much to figure out. For example, what's the real reason we're out here?"

"Don't change the subject, Mr. Slocum. We're talking about you."

"No, you are."

"All right, but I have my reasons. May I ask a question or two?"

"As long as you have your reasons," Slocum said dryly.

9

"Have you ever worked a cattle ranch?"

"Sure."

"I mean, more than a week or two at a time. Do you know your way around a cow?"

"If I remember right, the horns are on the front."

"Make all the jokes you like, Mr. Slocum, but don't expect me to laugh."

"I'm beginning to get that idea, Miss Anderson. It's just that most folks don't consider it any great sin to laugh. Or at least smile now and then."

Rachel Anderson sighed deeply and said, "Maybe not. But these days I don't really have much to smile about."

"Just what kind of trouble did I ride into?"

"Don't worry," she said with a sideways glance. "It's not your trouble. As long as you aren't a part of it, that is."

"I don't see how I could be, unless your trouble's in Chihuahua, which is where I spent most of the winter."

"Where you won the conchos," the woman mused. "And also where you managed to hang onto them. You know, Mr. Slocum, that didn't surprise me even a little bit. You have that certain look . . ."

The woman's voice trailed off as she studied Slocum, who waited a moment before he asked, "What kind of look is that?"

"It's hard to explain. Dangerous, maybe. Or at least alert. Like you generally know what's going on around you."

"If that's true," Slocum said with a smile, "it's not working today."

"I bet you can handle those guns pretty well."

Slocum shrugged. "I get along all right."

"How modest."

Slocum smiled again. He had lard on his lips and they were feeling a lot better. "Boasting can get you killed, Miss Anderson."

"Well, now . . . and level-headed too."

"Only when I'm sober."

"Have you by chance ever been a lawman?"

"Hardly."

Rachel Anderson turned sharply at the tone in his voice. "Is the law looking for you in New Mexico?"

"In New Mexico?" Slocum repeated with a grin. "Nope, not in New Mexico."

"I see."

They rode in silence for a minute or so, the sun burning their exposed skin and the wind-whipped dust biting at their faces. "Is it over?" Slocum said. "No more questions? You didn't even ask me how many men I've killed."

"Is that something you want to tell me?"

Slocum frowned at her, thinking once again about her age and deciding—as he looked at her in the sunlight—that his first impression had fallen short. She could already be nearing forty, and as far as he could tell she was alone. "What about you?" he said. "Have you ever been *off* this ranch?"

"Kevin has. That's my brother. He trailed a couple herds up to Abilene, back in the days before the railroad came through."

"You make it sound like his adventures were enough for both of you."

"I don't have to go anywhere. Everything I need is right here on the Lazy K."

"I see," said Slocum.

The woman jerked her head around as if to find out whether she was being mocked. A stiff gust of wind swept the bright red hair away from her face and Slocum was surprised by the depth of emotion in her dark eyes. He wasn't sure what it was, but it looked like something soft and painful showing through a crack in that hard-edged surface she liked to exhibit. It made Slocum sorry for his words, even though he still didn't believe her insistence that she was happy on the Lazy K. He rode in silence for several minutes, fascinated by this woman he couldn't understand, until he saw a familiar landmark.

"I found the calf over there," Slocum said, pointing. "Maybe fifty yards beyond the big yucca." Rachel Anderson reined in the grulla she was riding and Slocum stopped close beside her, forced by the grulla's size to look up at her from the back of his little Appaloosa. "I probably wouldn't have noticed him, except that I stopped to look."

"At what?"

"The yucca. It must be the biggest one I've ever seen." He was staring at it now, a trunk that looked as if it were made of dead leaves topped by a shower of fresh green spikes several feet above Slocum's head. Two thin stalks grew another twenty feet from the center of the spikes, ivory pods flowering at their tips as they swayed in the stiff desert breezes.

"Glad you like it," said the woman. "I'll tell you what. You sit there for a minute and enjoy the view while I take a look at something."

She turned her horse without waiting for an answer and Slocum watched with curiosity as she nudged the grulla into an easy lope, not toward the place where he had found the calf, but south along the trail. He noticed that she kept to the desert, riding parallel to the road for perhaps a quarter of a mile before she reined in again and slipped out of the saddle. She drew her Colt as her feet hit the ground, dropping to one knee to examine the road. Slocum saw her poke at something with her finger before she stood again and began walking slowly toward him, still looking at the trail.

Slocum frowned, finding it hard to accept the only possible explanation he could think of for Rachel Anderson's behavior. Why would she think it so important to check his story by examining the tracks on the trail?

He was aware that as she walked up the road, bent slightly forward, the revolver still in her hand, she was holding her eyes in such a way that she would be able to catch any sudden movement he made. She was also leading her horse on the off side, as if she thought he might take a shot at her and hoped to spoil his aim.

Slocum tried to carry that line of logic a little further, from the point of view of the woman on the road. What could make a man in his position want to kill Rachel Anderson? The answer to that seemed easy enough: because she was about to learn that his story of finding the calf had been a lie. But why would he have lied about it? The only answer to that one seemed to be that someone might use the calf to gain access to the house or the family. If that was true, then the Andersons had enemies, and the enemies were unknown to them. Slocum nodded quietly, feeling his resentment slip away. Then he had another thought that made his heavy black eyebrows bunch even tighter across the bridge of his nose.

The woman hadn't stopped to examine the prints his pony made before she rode away.

Slocum thought about that for a few seconds, troubled by the possibility that all his conclusions were false. He tried to think of any other series of explanations which might make sense. He realized very quickly that there were none, after which he thought once more about all the guesses he'd made.

Suddenly he smiled, feeling sure he knew the answer, and also with a growing admiration and respect for the woman.

He saw that she had stopped, squatting again to study the ground. Slocum watched her glance up at the yucca and then at him, and then return to her close, frowning examination of the trail. Slocum understood. He knew she had found the place where he'd stopped earlier that day to admire the big plant. His restless pony, pawing and stamping the ground, would have left a couple dozen prints in the loosely churned dirt before he guided it out across the hard-baked desert toward the calf. The woman straightened up, following that trail with her eyes for a moment before she holstered her gun and returned to Slocum.

"Just tell me one thing," Slocum said when she walked up, still leading her horse. "Which leg has the broken shoe?"

"The right foreleg," she said without hesitation. Then she grinned at him with an impish gleam in her eye. "Is your horse getting along all right?"

"You should have thought of that before we left the house," Slocum said. "That's when you checked my tracks, isn't it? When I headed over toward the water tank?"

The woman shrugged, her eyes still mischievous. "I figured you knew about the shoe, and that you could take care of your own horse."

"So you had this all planned out," Slocum said, shaking his head in wonder. "You thought I might be after something, and yet you came out here with me alone."

"I had to find out," the woman said grimly. "About you, and about the calf." The tightness went out of her face. "Besides, I was pretty sure your story would stand up. And if it did . . . well, I was hoping you could help me."

"Even so, you must be pretty sure of yourself with that Colt."

"I get along all right," said Rachel Anderson.

Slocum laughed, long and hard, hearing the echo of his own words. "I guess we're even on that one," he said. "What kind of help were you needing?"

"I'm not sure yet. I just know that that calf wasn't too far gone."

"Right again. This little pony had to do some pretty hard cutting just to run him down."

"Then the mother might still be alive, if we can find her. That's one of the things I was thinking."

"And the other?"

"Well," Rachel Anderson began, staring toward the horizon, "I was also thinking that if someone's taken her—the mother—then the trail would still be fairly fresh."

"And that's where I come in?"

Her eyes came back to him, with a pleading look. "I could pay you, if that's what you want."

"I wouldn't object to that. But why not just wait for your brother and your father?"

"They're way up north, branding." Slocum remembered the wistful way she had looked in that direction when he told her about the calf. "By the time I found them and brought them back it would be after dark. We'd be more than a day behind, at least."

"What about the law?" Slocum asked. "Where's the next town?"

Rachel Anderson nodded toward the northeast, her eyes clouding over with sadness, Slocum thought. "Chandlerville is just down the road from our ranch, right on the river, but I don't have much faith left in old man Wingfield."

"Who's he, the sheriff?"

The woman nodded. "For as long as I can remember. He and my father came into this country together, and I always thought he was the toughest man that ever lived —besides my father."

"Let's give him a chance, then."

"He's had dozens!" Rachel flared. "My father insists we report every loss to old Henry, and of course he does his duty every single time. Gets a posse together, rides to hell and back . . . and always comes back empty-handed. Except for excuses. He's got plenty of those, even though he never needed them before."

"Has he ever had a trail this fresh?"

"Not really," Rachel said with a frown, which suddenly disappeared beneath a look of determination. "But he still wouldn't, by the time we got him back here, and like I said, there was a time when he could have tracked a snake through hell. Look, Slocum, we're wasting daylight, and I've got a chance here that we've never had before. Are you coming with me or not?"

"The odds would sure be a lot better if we had some help."

"I thought so," the woman snapped. "You're worried about taking a girl along, aren't you?"

"That's not—"

"I suppose you think I should be home where I belong, baking those goddamn pies."

"I hope you didn't ruin them," Slocum said with a laugh, "but I'm not afraid you'll get underfoot out here."

The woman was glaring at him, trying to decide whether to believe him.

"Listen," Slocum said, "I'd probably rather have you riding with me than a lot of men I've come across. But I like to choose my fights, Miss Anderson, no matter who I'm riding with. And I sure as hell like to have something to say about the odds."

The woman stared up at him, hands propped on her hips, studying him for a moment with cold eyes. "Then it's money," she said scornfully, digging into a pocket of her jeans. "I thought of that too. If it's money you fight for, here's some payment on account."

Slocum looked at the twenty-dollar gold piece she held up to him, a dull yellow gleam in the desert sun, and then he looked at the veiled emotion burning in her eyes.

"Why don't we cross our bridges when we get to them," he finally said, ignoring the coin. "Let's just start looking for that cow, first off. Then, *if* we cut a trail that shouldn't be out here . . . well, we can see what the trail tells us and then we can figure out what makes the most sense." Slocum grinned at the woman. "More'n likely we'll just find a dead cow, and then we'll feel a little silly about all this talk."

Rachel Anderson slowly lowered her arm, looking confused, still watching Slocum as she stuffed the gold coin back in her pocket and climbed on the grulla with a graceful swing of long legs that Slocum appreciated. By the time she had adjusted herself in the saddle she had also managed to adjust the expression on her face. Once again Slocum saw only a cool, distant look, with no suggestion of appreciation.

"I suppose I have no choice but to go along," she said stiffly. "But I think we will find nothing more than the tracks of a missing herd, Mr. Slocum. If I'm right, I can only hope there's enough money to buy your loyalty."

Slocum took a breath and opened his mouth as if to speak, then couldn't imagine what he might say. He shivered suddenly in the desert sun with the strange and uncomfortable impression that he had lived this moment before, that he and Rachel Anderson had had this conversation in some other time. In the next instant he understood that he was remembering other women with this same fear of people, or perhaps simply of men. It was the distrust itself that was familiar, an expectation of the worst behavior and the meanest possible motives. There was a time when he might have talked to Rachel Anderson, hoping to soothe her fears, but now he had the benefit of his years and his experience and he understood that words wouldn't mean very much to her.

"Like I said," he repeated, "we'll cross that bridge when the time comes. Right now we're trying to figure out where the calf came from, and I can tell you that it was somewhere beyond that first ridge there. That's as far as I got before I quit. I can also tell you there weren't any cows grazing for at least a mile on the other side."

The woman stared west toward the ridge, bringing

her hand up to shade her eyes. Slocum looked at her hair and her long white fingers while she glanced thoughtfully toward the north and south, apparently fixing their position.

"There ought to be a deep wash over that way," she said after a minute. "You probably wouldn't have seen it from the ridge—this desert country can be tricky—but we've got a stock tank along in there somewhere."

"So let's see if the herd's gone to water, all right?"

"Sure," Rachel Anderson said grimly. "Let's see."

3

Slocum and the red-haired woman angled across a wide sweep of the New Mexican desert, two small riders who seemed lost under the great bowl of blue sky. But Rachel Anderson guided them directly to the stock dam that blocked the drainage against occasional rains, and there they found the evidence she seemed so sure they would find. In a ring of mud at the edge of the pond were the tracks of three shod horses that apparently had watered there.

"Early this morning, I think," Slocum said, squatting over the print of a horseshoe. He poked at the bottom of the print, then broke off a piece of drying mud from its rim and rolled the little brown ball between his fingers. "Possibly late yesterday afternoon, Miss Anderson, but I don't think any earlier than that."

"Then we've got them! Are you sure there were only three?"

"Unless one of them was using a horse that never needs water. Yeah, I only see three riders here. But they could be your own hands—"

"Every man on the place is up north with my father."

"—or they could have been passing through, heading somewhere else."

"And they just happened to stumble on this tank? Four miles from the trail, hidden down here in the wash?"

Slocum shrugged and Rachel Anderson leaned toward him, her eyes glistening as she shifted her weight restlessly from one foot to the other.

"This is our chance!" she told him. "The cows will leave enough of a trail for us to follow, and they'll slow down the bastards who are driving them." She shifted her weight again, with restless excitement. "We can catch them, Mr. Slocum! This is just what we've been praying for."

Slocum stared at her.

"I mean my family has. What's the matter, Mr. Slocum, aren't the odds good enough? There's only three men, you said—and maybe we can surprise them."

"No, the odds are fine."

"Then it's the payment," she said, reaching into her pocket. "I suppose you'll be wanting that double eagle now."

"That ain't it either," Slocum said. "Don't be so quick to give away your money."

"Then what's the matter?"

"Nothing I can put my finger on. I guess I'm still trying to figure you out."

"That can work both ways," the woman said, eyeing him carefully. "I find myself wondering, for example, why you don't want the gold. You must realize that I don't plan to pay you with . . . well, with anything besides money."

"Money will be just fine," Slocum said stiffly, "and I know where it'll be when the time comes." He showed her a sudden, wicked grin. "But if the time doesn't come, and I get myself shot, then you won't have to worry about digging it out of my bloody pocket."

Rachel Anderson shuddered. "That's not a cheerful thought."

"Yeah, but if I don't take your money then I can say what I want. And that's just the way I like it."

They let the horses drink their fill and then rode separate paths north and south in a great circle toward the west, and it was Rachel Anderson who again found the thing she had expected to find. She held her carbine high in the air and waved it back and forth until she knew Slocum had seen her signal. He cut directly toward her, his pony kicking up small puffs of dust that evaporated almost instantly in the stiff desert breeze.

There was no need for either of them to dismount to read the trail. They could see the broken branches of the sage and rabbit brush, the concentration of shallow nicks and scuffs in the sun-baked surface of the desert. Slocum satisfied himself by following the trail back toward the tank until it disappeared—where the grazing cows, widely scattered, would have been herded together—and returned to find Rachel Anderson shading her eyes and gazing off toward the west.

"I think they're heading for the mountains," she said with a frown. "If they get there before we do. . . ."

Slocum nodded as the woman's voice trailed off. "Our job would be a lot tougher," he agreed. "How far?"

"Twenty-five miles. Maybe only twenty from here."

Slocum sighed and said, "We've got a hard ride, then. Did you by any chance figure this thing far enough to bring some food in those saddlebags?"

"Of course," said the woman.

Slocum shook his head, grinning. "Of course," he echoed.

They delayed five minutes to gnaw on some jerked Rancho de Plata beef and empty one of the canteens they carried, then urged their mounts into an easy lope. Even slowing for a walk every hour to rest the horses, they were covering the miles at least twice as fast as the rustlers would be able to push their herd. If the outlaws had started that morning, then Slocum figured he and the woman could catch up with them by suppertime.

Otherwise they would meet sometime after dawn—*if* they decided it was safe to pursue the bandits into the mountains. Slocum smiled grimly when he thought of the possibility of battle, his blood racing and his muscles tightening with anticipation. He realized that his mostly peaceful winter in Chihuahua might have been too peaceful. Now he was itching for a fight, even grateful for the opportunity. He felt as if he were coming back to life.

The feeling faded slowly through the long afternoon, replaced by an aching of muscle and bone that grew into a steady throb of pain as he and the woman pushed toward the mountains. Anticipation faded as well, replaced by apprehension when the mountains loomed closer with no trace of the cattle. The foothills were only three miles away when Slocum spotted a light haze against the orange-red ball of the late afternoon sun. The dust appeared to be rising from behind a gentle slope of ground that hid the rest of the terrain between them and the mountains. There wasn't much question about what was stirring up the dust, however. Slocum glanced back at Rachel Anderson, who had already pulled her Winchester from its boot and now was studying the pall of dust. Slocum noticed that she was biting her lower lip, accentuating the downward turn at the corners of her mouth, and for a moment he forgot about the thieves beyond the ridge. She caught him staring at her, but she only assumed he was waiting for a signal.

"It's now or never," she said grimly.

"You figure on just charging over the rise?"

"I know it's not ideal—"

"That's putting it mildly."

"—but we don't have time for anything else. We can't let them get into those hills."

"Why not?" said Slocum. "I know it'll be harder to catch them if they do, but we could always pick up the trail in the morning. Cattle just don't move that fast."

The woman shook her head impatiently and said, "You don't understand, Mr. Slocum. We'd have no hope of following."

"Sure we would. We'd just—"

"Have you heard of Stonetown?"

That stopped Slocum short. He stared off over the hump of ground and said, "You mean the old mining town where . . ." He let his voice trail off when he saw Rachel Anderson nodding her head.

"There's an arroyo just over this rise," she told him, reining in her prancing horse. "It's the main pass over the mountains into Stonetown. Now can we go?"

Slocum sighed and, without another word, nudged his tired horse into a trot, gradually pushing the animal into a lope and then a run as they neared the top of the rise. In the back of his mind he was remembering some of the stories he'd heard about Stonetown, which was infamous along the border as a lawless nest of thieves and cutthroats. Some stories compared it to the Hole in the Wall up in Wyoming. He understood Rachel Anderson's concern for time, now. They might trail three rustlers up the canyon, only to meet a dozen outlaws on the other side. He glanced over at the woman, who was staying close, her red hair streaming back in the breeze. It blew into her mouth when she turned to face him.

"No killing unless you have to," she yelled, a little too loudly.

Slocum nodded, but Rachel Anderson was worried by the cold look in his eyes.

"I mean it, Mr. Slocum. Please!"

"I understand," he hollered over his shoulder. "You need someone who can point a finger."

The woman nodded, her dark eyes intent on Slocum for a moment longer before the two riders topped the ridge and turned their attention to the scene that appeared before them, between the ridge and the foothills.

The outlaws were less than a mile ahead, pushing a

small herd of maybe thirty or forty cattle. But they were also only two or three miles away from the mouth of the narrow canyon that Rachel had predicted they would see, cutting back into the mountains. The slopes began gentle and open enough, but Slocum could see several boulders not far in, great grey giants that could hide a small platoon, and beyond them a high outcropping of rock, gleaming a sharp white beneath the setting sun.

"Let's hope they don't see us right away," Slocum yelled to the woman. "That's our only . . . oh, shit."

The right flanker was yelling to the other two riders, waving his arms wildly toward Slocum and the woman on the ridge. The outlaw who was riding drag began racing back and forth behind the cattle, leaving puffs of smoke where he fired his revolver to spook them. Slocum heard one of the shots; the others were lost to the wind and the pounding of horses. The cattle, already nervous on this drive through strange territory, stampeded instantly, the two flank riders easing further off to the sides, just far enough to give them room while still guiding them gently toward the canyon.

No one had started shooting at anyone else yet. Slocum and the woman hadn't closed the gap to much less than half a mile—at least eight hundred yards. They were still gaining, running flat out, picking up a yard here and another yard there, but Slocum knew it wouldn't be enough. He was giving the chase every effort, the woman gamely keeping pace beside him, but only because he couldn't quit even when he knew he should. He was lashing his spent horse at the same time that he was thinking, *What the hell's the point?* He heard the pony's breath begin to rattle, and felt it almost as if his own lungs were giving out. He cursed again as he whipped the horse, feeling helplessly caught between his natural inability to quit and his certainty that the situation was hopeless.

Even so, they came close. The drag rider was less

than three hundred yards ahead when the bandits ran most of the herd up into the arroyo and turned off behind the boulders. Slocum eased up, veering off to the right to stay out of rifle range while his horse slowed to a walk.

Then he saw that Rachel Anderson was still running straight toward the arroyo.

"Hey!" Slocum yelled.

A puff of smoke appeared above one of the boulders, and a moment later a spout of dirt lifted several yards in front of the woman's horse. There was still no break in its stride. Slocum was already swinging back into line with the woman's path, kicking his pony desperately and taking off his hat to flail at its rump. The animal seemed to react to Slocum's sense of urgency, running even faster than it had before. There was more rifle fire from the boulders, the slugs now kicking up a steady pattern of dirt and gravel in front of both horses.

"Back off," Slocum yelled as he drew closer to the woman. "Don't be stupid, Rachel. Pull up."

"Get away!" the woman screamed over her shoulder. "Leave me alone." She was hugging the big grulla's neck, her face set in hard, grimly determined lines. "Get the hell away from me, Slocum!"

He had nearly pulled even with her again. "You'll get yourself killed, damn it. Give it up."

"No!"

"It's just a few cows!"

The woman gave him a look that was sadly helpless and scornful at the same time, as if it was Slocum who was missing the point. "Just get away!" she yelled again.

"I guess not," Slocum said under his breath. He lunged for a grip on her reins before she could react, wrapping them around his wrist and pulling hard. Her horse tried to shy away but gradually it yielded to Slocum's pressure, while he hunched his shoulders against the pounding of the woman's fists.

"God damn you!" she screamed, beating him. "Let me go."

Slocum only pressed his cheek against his shoulder and waited, aware that the firing from the boulders had already stopped. He figured the bandits had been trying to discourage pursuit more than anything, hoping they wouldn't have to murder anyone and get the situation more riled up than it already was. Now the rustlers were probably watching this little scene from their hiding place, waiting to see what might happen next.

What happened was that Rachel Anderson stopped hitting Slocum and started trying to pull the reins out of his hands, half-heartedly, an obvious exercise in futility. Then she slumped in the saddle, not moving at all, the reins apparently forgotten between her fingers. Slocum moved his horse a little closer and the woman leaned against him. Her body felt warm and her red hair was soft against his face.

"So close," she murmured.

"It's my fault," Slocum said, with real regret. "We might have had 'em if I hadn't spent so much time arguing with you."

"He'll never understand."

"Who won't?" said Slocum. "Your father? He'll think you did one hell of a job out here. It's only because of me that we didn't—"

"No, no," the woman cried bleakly. "He won't even approve of me coming out here." Her tone was turning bitter. "After all, it's not up to *me* what happens on the Lazy K."

"Why not?" said Slocum.

He felt the woman's body turn suddenly rigid, just before she pulled away from him to wipe her face on her dusty sleeve. It left muddy stains around her eyes, heightening their dark brown shade when she turned to stare at him for a moment. Then her eyes went to the arroyo and the boulders that hid the bandits, Slocum seeing only her profile and admiring the proud upturned chin.

"I'm sorry," the woman said stiffly, still gazing toward the horizon. "I quite forgot myself."

"Of course, Miss Anderson. Please don't—"

"We'll go back now, if you please."

She turned her horse, still without meeting Slocum's eyes, and set out toward home. Slocum watched her for a moment, then sighed deeply, shook his head, and began to follow.

4

The ranch buildings were dark, their stuccoed walls glimmering like pale ghosts under a half moon, when Slocum and Rachel Anderson dismounted wearily near the water tank. Slocum started feeling uneasy as soon as he stopped hearing the squeak of saddle leather, holding his breath in the desert silence to listen for any sounds that might signal a threat. He didn't hear any, and yet he still felt edgy. Then he realized that it was the absence of a particular sound that was making him nervous. There was no breeze at night to drive the windmill which loomed above them in the moonlight. Without the steady clanking of its blades and the sound of the saddle leather, the quiet peace seemed even deeper than it normally was. It made Slocum think of graveyards, and suddenly he shivered.

Rachel Anderson apparently misunderstood Slocum's moment of inactivity. "Isn't it wonderful," she whispered with deep feeling. "I don't think I could ever live without the stillness of the desert. The mystery."

Slocum frowned, studying the woman's outline in the dark. She had been about as quiet as the desert during their long ride back, discouraging all of Slocum's efforts to engage her in conversation. She had stopped her horse once, about half an hour after their confrontation with the rustlers, to stare longingly toward the mountains.

"I wish there was some way," she had murmured.

"They'd be expecting us, of course."

The woman had only scowled at Slocum and again nudged her horse into motion.

"That's not to say you can't get reinforcements and go back," Slocum had told her when he caught up. "Now that you know where to start looking. What's the big rush to get 'em tonight?"

Rachel Anderson had given him another look, one that he couldn't understand, after which she simply shook her head and turned away, making it obvious she wasn't going to offer an answer. The sun slipped behind the mountains half an hour after that and Slocum contented himself with enjoying the shifting colors of the long desert twilight. The last two hours of the ride were accomplished with the help of the early-rising half moon, Rachel Anderson confidently leading them toward her home while Slocum did little more than indulge in fantasies about what kind of bed she might provide for the rest of the night.

It surprised him to realize he wasn't including her in his thoughts, that he didn't even try to imagine her as part of the package. One reason was that he already felt tired enough to fall asleep in the saddle, which he came close to doing once or twice. But it was also obvious to Slocum that he had no hope of sleeping with Rachel Anderson. He'd spent nearly ten hours with her by now, and never had he seen even a hint that she might be interested in him. In fact, everything pointed the other way. She didn't like Slocum, she didn't trust him, and she was immune to any efforts to change her mind.

That was why her sudden intimacy seemed doubly surprising. Perhaps the woman had simply been caught up in her love for the desert night, momentarily forgetting to be suspicious. Or perhaps she truly felt that Slocum was sharing her enjoyment of the silence. It left him wondering what he should say. He didn't want to spoil this unexpected moment, but he also had a lot of faith in her ability to know a line of crap when she heard it. For the time being he said nothing, taking her reins and leading both of their horses the last few feet toward the water tank.

"I'm sorry," Slocum told her then. "The desert is a fine place to be, but that's not what I was thinking about."

"Oh?" said the woman, stepping back and narrowing her eyes. "Just what was on your mind, then?"

"Christ!" Slocum snarled. "Don't flatter yourself. I was just thinking, for a minute there, that it was *too* quiet."

"No big mystery in that," the woman said defiantly. "You were probably missing the sound of the windmill."

"I know that!"

Slocum was suddenly aware of the controlled fury in his voice, and the savage flaring of temper that had put it there. The intensity of his feelings didn't make sense. He took a deep breath, squeezing his eyes closed for a moment, then tried again.

"I'll tell you what," he said quietly. "Why don't you go ahead and give me that double eagle now, and I'll be on my way."

The woman seemed confused. "You mean leave? Right now?"

"The sooner the better."

"But where will you sleep?"

"Out there somewhere." He lifted his chin, using it to point north, and nearly smiled with a sudden thought. "Where I can enjoy the peace and quiet of the desert," he said with deliberate slowness.

Rachel didn't smile, but Slocum hadn't really expected her to. He was aware only of a little less rigidity in her body.

"No," she said, almost as if she were speaking to herself, "that's not right. The least I can do is offer you a clean bed."

"That's not necessary—"

"When was the last time you slept between sheets, Mr. Slocum?"

"Real linen?" he asked.

"And don't forget those pies I was baking."

"You sure are being nice all of a sudden. Why the cordial treatment?"

The woman had been using a light, teasing tone. Now she tilted her head slightly, her eyes fixed on Slocum's face, and turned serious. "Every now and then I take a chance—like the chance that you might be a good man."

"Well, golly, thanks."

"Don't be that way, Mr. Slocum. Surely you're aware of the nature of most of your fellow riders on the grubline."

"Yeah," Slocum admitted. "But you take a hell of a long time to make up your mind."

"I suppose I don't flatter myself as a very good judge of character."

"No?" said Slocum, raising an eyebrow.

Rachel shook her head.

"Well, maybe," said Slocum, changing his mind. "Maybe you're too busy expecting the worst of everyone to trust your woman's intuition."

Rachel stiffened again. "I'm glad you have it all figured out."

"You're right," Slocum said with a shrug. "It's none of my business. Please accept my apologies."

There was another short silence, filled with the sloppy sound of the horses still sucking water from the tank. Rachel Anderson seemed to relax again, almost in spite of herself. Slocum couldn't really tell what was different about her—he couldn't see much in the dim glow of the half moon—but it was something he could feel. The changes in her mood seemed to produce changes in his. A moment before he had wanted to be anywhere else; now he wanted to take two steps forward and gather her in his arms. There was a pounding in his chest and a painful swelling in his trousers.

"Well," said Rachel, spinning suddenly on her feet. "We can't let these poor animals bloat themselves, can we?" She patted the big grulla's neck, tugging at its reins until it backed reluctantly away from the water tank. Slocum watched her for a moment, then shook his head in exasperation—a feeling he was getting used to by now—and followed suit. They stripped the saddles from their horses and watched the big animals roll in the dirt, listening to the heavy grunts and feeling the sharp sting of dust in their nostrils.

Rachel avoided Slocum's eyes, even when they led their ponies toward the dark mouth of the barn. Slocum held back when he saw her fumbling with something on the wall just inside the opening, then continued a moment later when he saw the flare of a lucifer. By the time he got inside a coal-oil lantern was casting its murky yellow glow over the stacked bales of hay extending down one side of the barn, and the line of stalls on the other side. Slocum and the woman heaved their saddles onto the edge of one of the stalls, which reminded Slocum of something he hadn't thought of all day.

"I guess it'll be a while longer till we have that pie," he told the woman.

He half expected another show of suspicion, but all he got was curiosity. "Why is that?" she said.

"That calf I brought in today. We never did get its mama."

Rachel closed her eyes and groaned softly. "I almost wish you hadn't remembered," she said, her voice blurred with exhaustion. "But of course I'm glad you did."

"I saw a cow in the corral, didn't I?"

"That old—" she began, then stopped herself. "I'll go get her, if you wouldn't mind putting up the horses."

Slocum took her horse's reins and led their horses to separate stalls, then found a grain bin and dumped a shovelful in for each horse. He also dumped a shovelful into a pail and set in on the ground in front of what he assumed was a milking stool. A big Hereford ambled out of the night a moment later and headed straight for the pail, making a loud snuffling sound that echoed through the tin. Rachel followed the cow in, glancing at the pail and giving Slocum a speculative look before she reached another bucket down off a nail and sat beside the cow. He heard the sharp streams of milk hitting the side of the bucket as he headed back down the line of stalls.

The calf offered no resistance when Slocum picked it up, and he came back with its head rolling loosely over the side of his arm. "This may take a little doing," he said to Rachel. "I hope that cow doesn't mind adopting."

"This damn cow never makes anything easy," the woman said. "Hang onto the calf for a second."

Rachel reached behind her back for a short chain with a metal clamp on each end, which she slipped over the narrow shanks of the cow's hind legs. The cow immediately raised one leg and then the other, trying to remove the clamps, but they stayed tight, restricting the movement of her legs. Slocum nodded his satisfaction and tried to prop up the calf beneath her, but the calf's legs folded up and it flopped on the ground.

"I know just how it feels," Rachel sighed.

Slocum grinned at her, then snaked one hand beneath the calf while he grabbed its head with the other. "Come on," he urged, lifting the calf toward the cow's bag. "It's all yours. A regular feast."

The calf closed its eyes. Slocum was moving its head so that its lips brushed the cow's teats, but the calf didn't show any interest. The cow came to life, though, swinging her big head back to sniff at the little calf

being forced on her. Immediately she was trying to kick
it away, instinctively saving her milk for the calf she
didn't have anyway. When the kick chain hampered her
efforts she tried to move off, but she found she couldn't
walk any easier than she could kick. She swung her
head around once again, perhaps with the idea of using
it to shove the intruder out of the way, but Slocum
yelled at her and threatened her with an upraised hand.
It was probably nothing more than a case of nerves that
made her do what she did next, but it seemed like pure
mean stubbornness. Slocum and the woman both half
expected it, fortunately, so they were ready to back
away fast when the cow lifted her tail.

"You ornery son of a bitch!" Slocum complained. "If
you were mine I'd be butchering you right now." Rachel
Anderson laughed suddenly, and Slocum joined in after
a moment. "That's the worst-smelling cow I've ever
come across," he said.

"I'm sure," said the woman, still chuckling. "But
she's all we've got."

Slocum shook his head in disgust and tried again.
Now he worked his hand up under the calf's jaw, using
thumb and middle finger to force it open so that he
could maneuver the calf's mouth over one of the nipples. But the calf simply let the nipple slip out of its
mouth as soon as the cow tried to shift away to the side.

"Here," said Rachel, "let's try this." She grasped a
teat in one hand and placed her other hand over Slocum's to guide the calf's mouth while she squeezed.
Slocum still held its jaws apart, so that she could aim
the stream of warm milk inside. Most of it poured down
over Slocum's hand—and the woman's—but some of it
seemed to be trickling down the calf's throat.

Slocum was looking at Rachel's hand on his, feeling
her warmth at the same time that he felt the sticky
warmth of the milk. He glanced up at her, squatting
next to him, and found her watching him. She quickly

looked away and withdrew her hands.

"Let's see if it's gotten the idea," she said quietly.

Once again Slocum lifted the calf's head toward the bag, and once again it ignored the nipples. Its head lolled listlessly to one side.

"Damn!" said Rachel.

Slocum eased the calf back to the ground and stared at it for several seconds, stroking its neck, feeling sorry for something so helpless and also trying to understand what it might need. Something made him glance at Rachel again, and again he found her staring at him. And again she looked away.

Slocum dredged up another idea from his memory. He squeezed a little milk on his index finger and slipped it into the calf's mouth. At first there was no response, but Slocum waited, still stroking the calf's neck. Then he felt a slight pressure on his finger. He pulled his finger out, squirted more milk on it, and put it back between the calf's teeth. This time he felt a distinct sucking pressure, the teeth digging into his skin. He yanked his hand away, but when he looked at Rachel he was grinning. So was she.

"Let's try again," he said.

The calf still refused to stand on its own legs, but now it made feeble sucking noises when Slocum held its mouth up against one of the cow's teats. At first Slocum wasn't even sure the calf was squeezing hard enough to get any milk, but gradually the noises got louder and after a minute or two the calf was pulling and tugging at the nipple. The cow was still trying to kick the calf, and move away from it, and push at it with her head, but Rachel discouraged the cow while Slocum worked to keep the calf within easy reach. The calf was sucking greedily now, even knocking the bag with its head to keep the milk coming down. Rachel laughed, with a small choking noise at the end, her eyes shining as she flashed Slocum another look.

It wasn't long before the calf had had its fill, and refused to take any more milk. It was able to stand on wobbly legs now, but it collapsed as soon as it tried to walk. Slocum scooped the calf up in his arms while Rachel moved her bucket back underneath the cow.

"I'll finish her off," she said. "And maybe she'll allow us to sleep a little later tomorrow."

Slocum carried the calf into the dark shadows of its stall about halfway down the barn, closed the gate on his way out, and immediately sank into a pile of loose straw on top of several bales stacked on the opposite side. He closed his eyes for a moment, enjoying the dusty smell of the hay and the sound of milk squirting into the pail. He was drifting somewhere between sleep and wakefulness, dimly aware that the sound of milking had stopped after a while, followed by a brief silence. Perhaps the woman was looking at him, wondering what to do. Then he heard her walking toward him and he opened his eyes to see the soft curves of her body outlined against the yellow light of the lantern. She stood over him for a moment, the expression on her face hidden in shadow. Slocum was about to struggle to his feet when she sank down beside him.

5

"You look worn out," Rachel said.

"It's been a long day. For both of us."

Slocum had a feeling that their words were just words, not meaning much, or at least not saying what they really wanted to say. He sat up slowly, bringing his face closer to hers, aware of a flushed, fluttering sensation, the kind that usually means the other person is feeling the same thing. There was something about the silence, the deep shadows at this end of the barn, the distant flickering light, the weariness melting in their bones . . .

She had not moved away, and their faces were only inches apart.

"You've been a big help," Rachel whispered.

Slocum nodded. "I'll go through hell for a piece of fresh pie."

The woman smiled for an instant and then looked serious again, her eyes fixed on Slocum's. He was aware that their faces were drifting closer together, but he wasn't sure which one of them was moving. Maybe they both were. Her eyes closed just before they kissed, lids squeezing together as if something pained her. Slocum resisted a sudden wild hunger, a desire to throw her onto the hay and drive himself into her. His instinct told him to make no sudden moves, to treat the woman the same way he would approach a skittish horse or a wounded animal.

The kiss lingered, long and soft. She broke away once, looked Slocum in the eye, then took a deep breath and kissed him again. Immediately he felt more heat in the breath that touched his cheek, felt her breasts rising and falling against his chest. He put his arms around her and felt her mouth fall open beneath his, their lips grinding urgently together and their tongues meeting. Slocum's hands found a patch of bare flesh where the woman's blouse had pulled out of her jeans. He pulled at the blouse some more and Rachel squirmed beneath his touch, pressing herself against him and moaning softly when he slipped one hand behind her and down her jeans.

The woman was using her own hands to unbutton his shirt, rubbing the thick black hair that covered his chest, her hand moving in wider and wider circles until it brushed the bulge in his trousers. The hand moved away, then came back.

Some part of Slocum's mind was still working—barely—trying to connect the distant and suspicious woman he'd gotten used to with this hungry and demanding woman whose need seemed to be as great as his own. It occurred to him that her need might even be greater. He had enjoyed plenty of willing women during the winter months in Chihuahua, after all, while Rachel Anderson had apparently spent the winter—and probably her whole life—wasting away at the Lazy K. There wouldn't be more than a few men available, and none of them likely to make any headway against all the roadblocks she would throw down in front of them. Not one of them, he thought with an inward smile, would have had the lucky break of an orphan calf to take care of.

There wasn't much more room for Slocum's thoughts. They were breaking up and scattering as Rachel fumbled with the buttons of his trousers. He in turn was tugging her jeans down over the fine swell of her hips, noticing how white her skin looked against the straw, and how it seemed to shimmer in the edges of the light that reached them from the lantern. The woman's long legs fell open as soon as they were free of the jeans, spreading wide, and Slocum covered with his hand the thick patch of hair between them. She writhed beneath his touch.

Rachel gasped, then began to push herself down on Slocum's fingers, grinding faster and faster, hanging onto him and sucking at his lips when she wasn't struggling to breathe. Suddenly she was crawling on top of him, pushing him farther back into the hay as she lowered herself onto him, guiding him with her hands. He felt her muscles gripping his shaft as she moved above him, sliding along its full length.

Slocum reached up now and unbuttoned Rachel's blouse, watching her breasts fall free and begin to sway as she rocked back and forth. He took one breast in each hand and squeezed them, rolling them together and rolling her nipples between his fingers, enjoying the way her breasts swelled out and overflowed his hands. Rachel cried out suddenly, rocking even more wildly, her head thrown back so that her throat was one straight line from chest to chin, shining with sweat. She whimpered and groaned and suddenly she was arching her back, not breathing, Slocum feeling himself clamped tight as if he were in a vice. He squeezed her breasts again, thrust himself harshly up inside her, and felt his own back go rigid as he exploded with a fierce feeling of release. A shudder swept across his skin and then he settled back, still feeling himself being milked inside her. In the next instant she collapsed on top of him, holding his head between her arms and showering his face with kisses.

Slocum lay still, a nerveless exhaustion pouring back through his body. It was almost a feeling of paralysis, as if he couldn't move a muscle even if he wanted to.

Rachel gradually stopped kissing him, still lying on top, and for a while he thought she had fallen asleep. He was almost asleep himself when she murmured, "Now you know."

Slocum opened his eyes, blinking against the sandy burning sensation. "Know what, Rachel?"

"Why I acted like I did before." She sniffed, and just then Slocum felt dampness on his cheek. "I can't help myself. I just can't . . . can't stop, once the desire is in me." She buried her head against Slocum's neck, crying brokenly.

It was Slocum's turn to be wary, to feel suspicion, mixed with a tentative pity stirred by the woman's tears. "I don't understand," he said carefully. "Why is it something you want to fight?"

"Of course you don't understand. You just had a great time, didn't you?"

"I thought you did too."

Rachel rolled off to the side and curled up, hugging herself. "You can leave any time you want," she said harshly.

"Is that what you want?"

"It's what *you* want. I know. Just to get away as fast as possible."

Slocum studied her, his eyebrows bunching together in a frown. "Maybe you've been losing control with some of the wrong people, Rachel."

"Well it's not likely to happen with another woman, now, is it?"

"I hope not," Slocum said with a smile. "But not all men are alike."

"Hah!"

Slocum frowned again and said, "That's a hard argument to answer." He moved closer to her and tried to put his arms around her, but her body remained rigid beneath his touch and she refused to meet his eye. "You know," he said lightly, "pretty soon I'll be so mad that it'll cancel out how much I enjoyed what we just did. Will you be happy then?"

That at least got her to look at him, although he couldn't tell whether she appreciated the remark. He was hoping for a softening in her eyes, maybe even the hint of a smile. Instead he saw them go wide with a sudden look of horror, just as he became aware of the distant plodding of hooves and snorting of horses. Rachel's mouth fell open and her hand came to her throat.

"Oh my God," she wailed. "It's my father!"

This all seemed a little too familiar to Slocum, this business of a man and a woman hopping around and pulling their clothes on, both of them eyeing the door while they fumbled with their buttons. It was true that this time they had both been partially dressed to begin with, and there were no bedsheets to straighten out, but they did have to do something about the bits of straw clinging stubbornly to their clothes and in their hair. The stems seemed too numerous to attack one by one, and yet they survived several attempts at a quick brushing.

"I don't understand this," Rachel whispered hoarsely. "He wasn't supposed to be home until— How do I look now?"

"Here," said Slocum, "turn that way a minute. Good. Are you sure it's your father?"

"Who else would be riding in here at . . . It's nearly midnight, isn't it? They must have finished after lunch and decided they could make it back with the moonlight."

"Your enemies wouldn't be this bold, then?"

"They haven't been so far. Wait, you've got a few pieces on your shoulder. There. Are you sure I look all right?"

"Good Lord," Slocum said, "this is just your father coming up the road, not your husband. And you are a bit older than twenty-one, aren't you?"

"Don't remind me," Rachel said, rolling her eyes. "Just wait till you meet my father. Then you'll understand."

Slocum nodded, thinking that he might understand a lot more than Rachel's sudden attack of nerves. "Might as well get it over with," he said. "What's your father's name?"

"Foley. Kevin's my brother."

They watched from the barn for a minute or two to make sure, Slocum easing his Colt Navy out of its holster because he felt better with its ivory grips cool in his palm. But the procession came on slowly and doggedly, with no sense of the furtive excitement that would animate bandits on the prowl, only weariness. Slocum counted a total of ten riders. Rachel very quickly recognized her father's horse and then her father in the pale light. She said he was in the lead, just ahead of her brother. She carried the lantern out to meet them at the water tank, Slocum following a step or two behind.

The man in the lead was not a big man. Foley Anderson wouldn't have been readily noticeable among his vaqueros except for some quality that had nothing to do with his physical size. Slocum saw it immediately— whatever it was—even in the moonlight. Something about the way he carried himself, perhaps, with a straight-backed stiffness that smacked of a military bearing. Perhaps it was nothing more than supreme self-assurance. Slocum didn't try to describe it to himself as he stood there waiting, didn't try to give it a name. He simply eyed the old rancher appraisingly and realized that he would have recognized him as the boss even if he had not been the one to stop his horse directly in front of Rachel, the other riders bunching up behind him. He nodded down at her, glanced at Slocum, then turned back to his daughter.

"What's going on?" he said.

"I'm afraid we've had another loss," Rachel said. "Mr. Slocum here was kind enough to—"

"Another loss?" said the rancher, his eyes flicking to Slocum and back again. "When?"

"I'm afraid so. They took about forty head. But we almost had them! If only we'd been—"

"You *saw* them?" demanded Rachel's brother. He was nudging his horse awkwardly out of the shadows behind their father, a hulking figure who looked uncomfortable in the saddle, but managed to look vaguely menacing as well. "You mean to say you actually saw the rustlers?"

"Three of them, Kevin. We were less than half a mile away when they got into some rocks and we had to give up. They were heading straight for Stonetown."

"Holy Christ," said Kevin Anderson.

"We?" said his father, looking at Slocum again. "Do you mean to say that you chased after the outlaws with this . . ."

"John Slocum," Rachel said as her father let his voice trail off. "He made the discovery that led—well, indirectly—to my discovery of the missing animals."

"Good Lord, Rachel, why didn't you just come find me?"

"You were so far away, and the trail was so fresh. I thought it would be our best chance to—"

"Get yourself killed," the old man nearly shouted. "How stupid can you be, girl? The whole thing could have been a trap."

"Maybe still is," muttered Kevin, eyeing Slocum. "For all we know."

"I took precautions," Rachel said plaintively, with a timidity that surprised and disappointed Slocum, and helped make him even madder than he already was. "I was being careful."

"Careful!" roared Foley Anderson. "What's careful about chasing outlaws all over the desert when you're not only outnumbered, but all you've got is some unknown saddle bum to keep you company?"

"Did you build this ranch by being careful?" said Slocum.

There was a sudden hushed silence, the rancher staring down from the saddle like a king from his throne. "What do you mean by that?" he said coldly.

"I mean you're not giving your daughter near enough credit," Slocum said, breathing evenly and working to control himself. "She knew just what she was doing today."

"Well, now, I'm just pleased as hell to have your opinion."

"I don't give a damn whether you're pleased or not," Slocum said, a sharper edge coming into his voice.

"Hey!" Kevin said. "You can't—"

"With two or three minutes' difference in our timing," Slocum continued, pointedly ignoring the hulking man beside his father, "you'd be thanking us for saving those cows instead of embarrassing your daughter."

Kevin Anderson started yelping with indignation again, but the old man held up his hand to cut him off, never taking his eyes off Slocum. But his gaze was more thoughtful now, and his tone not as blustery. "If you were around to thank, Mister—Slocum, is it? More likely I'd be out there diggin' a grave for my only daughter."

"No," Slocum said slowly, looking at Rachel. "If there were any graves to be dug, I think they'd've been for the rustlers." The woman had been staring at him with her eyes wide and her beautiful mouth hanging partially open, as if she couldn't believe the way he was treating the men in her family. Now she closed her mouth, with a new expression that seemed to soften her eyes. Slocum even thought she might have been standing a little straighter, but maybe it was a trick of the flickering lanternlight. "Anyway," he added, "she obviously can take care of her herself."

"She can ride and she can shoot," the old man admitted, betraying a hint of pride. "I was teaching her everything I knew, until my wife finally gave me a son." He leaned his head briefly toward Kevin, but he was still eyeing Slocum, his interest apparently triggered by the look that had passed between his daughter and the stranger. He was studying them in thoughtful silence, letting his instincts tell him whatever they were sharp enough to tell.

Slocum's first instinct was to get the hell out of there, remembering his earlier thoughts about messing around with tough ranchers' daughters, but when he took a closer look it didn't seem like there was any threat in Foley Anderson's steady gaze. The whole family was full of surprises.

"Maybe you'd better just tell me the story," the rancher said to Slocum. "Rachel, why don't you get some coffee on the stove while we put up the horses."

"But, Father—"

"You've done a good job," Anderson said soothingly. "Don't think I don't appreciate it. But now we're back and we can take care of things. You just scoot along and get the place in order, all right?"

Slocum was watching Rachel, still half expecting a protest of some kind, but this was not the same cool and level-headed woman who had confronted him with a Winchester at noon. She only nodded and said, "Yes, sir," in a tone that was more sadly resigned than defeated. She gave Slocum one last look before she moved off toward the dark house.

He watched her for a moment longer, feeling a little sad himself at first, and then feeling the sadness turn slowly back into anger as his attention focused itself once again on the rancher. But Foley Anderson was easing himself very tenderly out of the saddle, staggering slightly once his feet were on the ground, and suddenly it was hard to think of him as a tyrant. He was only an old man who had spent too many years in the saddle and had probably broken too many bones. He had a sort of rolling, bowlegged walk that looked painfully stiff through the knees. Slocum caught himself wincing once or twice in sympathy as he followed Anderson and the other riders toward the water tank.

"I guess it's been a long day for all of us," Slocum said, over the sound of six horses greedily sucking up water. "But the reason you found me here is that I happened to run across one of your calves—"

"That can wait," Foley Anderson said abruptly. "Kevin, take care of my horse. Mr. Slocum? Let's head on up to the house."

Slocum nodded warily and fell in beside the rancher, who said nothing for several seconds and then stopped suddenly about halfway between the windmill and the ranch house. The two men faced each other in the moonlight, Foley Anderson standing back and tilting his head up to stare into Slocum's eyes. *Shit,* thought Slocum, *here it comes.* He listened to the steady whistling noise of the old man's breathing, and he waited.

"Did you know my daughter before today?" Anderson said almost immediately.

"Know her?" said Slocum, a little puzzled. "We just met, sir, when I brought in the calf I started telling you about."

"Just met," echoed the rancher, as if he, too, was puzzled. "Of course, you spent the whole day together."

"Well . . . yeah. Out on the trail."

"Anything happen after you got back?"

Slocum was ready with a denial, but he hesitated just an instant to consider what kind of traps could be waiting somewhere down the line. The hesitation saved him from having to answer at all.

"Well, hell," said Anderson, "I guess that ain't none o' my business, strictly speaking. She's old enough. Let's just say I wouldn't be surprised if—well, damn it, the thing is I *would* be surprised. That daughter of mine scares the men off faster than a squaw with the cholera. But you"—Anderson seemed to stare hard at Slocum in the moonlight—"somehow I think you got to her."

Slocum stood frozen. He'd felt a moment of relief, followed immediately by an even greater wariness. The old man was just like his daughter: you could never guess what either one of them might say next. Slocum didn't say anything at all. He was barely breathing.

"Well, even if you didn't get her down in the hay—" Anderson said impatiently.

Slocum choked back a cough.

"—I'll be damned if I don't think she's ripe for it."

Slocum stared down at him.

"What I'm trying to say is, have at her, Slocum! With my blessing. The poor girl is drying up and going to waste out here and it hurts me to see it and there ain't a damn thing I can do about it. She's thirty-eight next month. She needs to make a family."

Slocum just listened.

"Yeah," said the rancher, "I can see that you ain't exactly the family type. You got a burr under your saddle. But think about it, Slocum. This is the thing I'm really trying to say. Anybody who winds up marrying my Rachel, he won't be sorry."

"He won't?" said Slocum.

"He'll have cows, Slocum! And a place of his own to run 'em. Maybe even with a little operating capital thrown in."

"You're trying to *buy* a husband for Rachel?" Slocum said incredulously.

"A girl that looks like that? She could have any man in the state. It's just that she doesn't generally return their interest. Now it looks like she's gone and gotten sweet on a drifter—no offense, Slocum—so I figure it's my duty as a father to offer . . . well, an incentive. I'm trying to make you think a little harder about planting your boots in one place, for a change."

"Less than twelve hours after I met your daughter?"

"How long were you planning to stick around?"

Slocum shrugged.

"I thought so. Look, Slocum, I'm an old man, and maybe that makes me impatient. When you get to be my age you start realizing that you're running out of time. I'm tired of waiting to see what happens. So, will you think about it?"

Slocum shook his head and sighed. "What a day," he said, and then, "You know, Mr. Anderson, it seems to me you'd want to keep Rachel around so she could run the ranch—you know, later on."

"After I die, you mean."

"Well, yeah."

"That'll be Kevin's department. He's my son, and the truth is, Slocum, I'd rather have Rachel concentrating on something else."

"You don't think she'd do a good job?"

"I won't say that. She has a good idea now and then. But her ideas and Kevin's ideas . . ."

"Aren't the same," Slocum finished, nodding with comprehension.

"Not by a mile, Slocum. So there's something for you to sleep on tonight."

Slocum sighed deeply, seeing images of the day—and the night—flicker through his head. "I appreciate your concerns," he said, "and I admit I couldn't hope to wind up with anyone prettier'n your daughter . . ."

"But the burr is still there," said Anderson, taking a turn at finishing one of Slocum's thoughts.

"Yeah," Slocum said uncomfortably, "that's mostly true—"

"Well, hell, I couldn't expect it to be any different for you than it was for me at your age."

"—but I also think you got an exaggerated notion of how close I am to your daughter."

The rancher stared at Slocum for a moment in silence, then made a sound of disgust and started off toward the house again, shaking his head. "Chases 'em all off," the old man murmured sadly. "Why the hell does she chase 'em all away?"

Slocum, hurrying to keep up, didn't have any answers.

6

There was a fire blazing away in the big cast-iron stove when Slocum followed the old rancher into the kitchen. Anderson went to stand in front of the stove itself, rubbing his hands together, while Slocum stopped just inside the door, hat in hand, and glanced toward Rachel working at a sideboard. She stood with her back to the room, her thick red hair gleaming softly in the glow from several candles, and after a few seconds Slocum realized she wasn't planning to turn around right away. She was busy cutting something, and probably using that as an excuse. He wondered whether she was more afraid of looking at him or at her father.

"Nothing like a fire on one of these chilly desert nights," Anderson told Slocum with a grin. "It takes some of the ache out of my old bones."

"It would also help if you stopped going out on all the roundups," Rachel said to the wall, still bent over her task at the sideboard.

The old man winked at Slocum, his grin getting wider. "My loving daughter doesn't think I should work so hard," he said. "She thinks I should take life easier."

"You've certainly earned it," the woman said sharply. Slocum heard the clinking of silverware just before she turned around and caught his eye, with a look that was both angry and pleading. "I'd say fifty years of hard

50

work is enough, wouldn't you?" She looked at her father. "You've already broken your left knee twice and your right one three times. Are you waiting for one knee to catch up with the other?"

"Yep," said the old man, "she just wants me to set out on the porch and wait my time." A sudden dark look crossed his face, and his tone turned heavy with sarcasm. "Of course, she doesn't know what I ought to *do* with all that time."

"Don't make fun of me," the girl begged. "I'm just worried about you."

"There's no need for that," Anderson said impatiently.

Slocum heard the pounding of boots coming through the house.

"But, Father, it's not as if you don't have someone who can look after the place for you. Why take so many risks if you—"

"Oh, Christ," said a voice behind Slocum. "Are we back to this?"

Slocum saw the flare of anger in Rachel's eyes just before he turned to get a better look at Kevin Anderson, who nearly filled the doorway, framed by heavy wooden beams. Slocum realized he was younger than Rachel by several years.

"You should be backing me up," Rachel said to her brother. "What if he gets thrown again? What if a horse falls on him? He just can't take the chances he used to."

Kevin Anderson only shrugged, showing a small impatient scowl. "I figure he's a grown man and he can do whatever he wants," he said, as if the subject bored him. "Say, do I smell fresh-baked pie?"

The girl stared at her brother for a moment, then looked at her father and Slocum in turn, her eyes glistening, before she turned back to the sideboard to finish her cutting. The old rancher winked at his son this time, as the two men sat down at a table covered with yellow oilcloth. Slocum joined them reluctantly, thinking that a cold camp out in the desert would have been a hell of a lot more enjoyable than a warm kitchen with this particular family. He noticed that Rachel kept her distance from him as she slapped tin plates and forks down in front of the men, each plate nearly covered by a generous chunk of peach pie. She had put down tin cups and was pouring coffee when Kevin Anderson spit his first bite back onto his plate.

"This is awful," he said. "What the hell happened?"

"Well," Rachel stammered, "they were still baking when Mr. Slocum rode in with the calf, and from the story he told . . . well, I wanted to leave right away, while the trail was still fresh."

"So you let the pies turn to mush?"

"It was an emergency, Kevin. I had to put out the fire but I left the pies in, hoping they'd bake enough with the leftover heat."

"Well, they didn't. You might as well throw them all out."

"Not so fast," Slocum said, forcing an easy smile. "This may not be what you boys are used to, but it's still better than anything I've had all winter. Would you kindly set those pies aside for me, Miss Anderson? And maybe the hands down in the bunkhouse?"

The girl flashed him a grateful look while Kevin's expression turned sour.

"Nothing doing," said the old rancher. "This tastes just fine to me." He cut out a second bite. "But, Rachel . . . no more running off, okay?"

"Why not?" said the girl, almost defiant now. "It's just what you would have done, isn't it?"

"That's a different story—"

"We have to stop them before they bleed us dry, don't we? We never had a fresh trail before, because those bastards always manage to hit us right where there's nobody around."

"Now just calm down," said the old man. "We'll catch those fellas."

"Before we go bankrupt or after?"

Anderson's face hardened into the kind of expression that must have made his enemies think twice over the years. "First of all," he said coldly, "no one said a thing about letting the operation go under. You oughta have more faith than that in your old man. Second of all, you shouldn't get so worked up about something that's really none of your business. Or our guest's."

"None of my business!"

"Rachel—" said Kevin.

"Your rightful place is in another man's home," the old man broke in, "takin' care of him and giving me grandkids that I can bounce on my knee. That would be a lot more pleasing to me than if you captured *twenty* rustlers."

"But I don't want—"

"Naturally, Rachel, until that day comes, you're perfectly welcome to live here." The old man grinned again, glancing at Kevin. "I have to admit I'm glad we're eating her cooking instead of ours, right, son?"

The younger Anderson shrugged his massive shoulders, poking at his pie with his fork. "Most of the time," he said.

The old rancher laughed at that and looked at Slocum to include him in the joke, never seeing the anguish in his daughter's eyes. Slocum kept his face blank, refusing to laugh at Rachel's expense but also unable to show her any of the things he truly felt. He wanted to tell her his own story, tell her what it was like to be forced off the farm where he and his father and his father's father had been born, just because a corrupt carpetbagging judge fancied himself a horse breeder. Then it came to him that it was probably even more painful for the girl, whose own father and brother were telling her that she could not expect to remain forever in the only home she'd known—that she was nothing better than a guest there. Slocum noticed that her lower lip was trembling slightly, and admired her all the more when she pushed on.

"What do you plan to do?" she asked quietly.

"About the cattle?" said the old man.

"Will you be following the trail?"

The rancher looked at his son, who shrugged again and said, "They'll be long gone by tomorrow."

"But it's the best chance we've had, Kevin. And the rustlers were heading for that canyon even before they knew we were there."

Both father and son looked to Slocum for confirmation.

"I don't know why you can't take her word for it," he told them. "But she's right. They were making a beeline all afternoon."

"I keep thinking maybe they've got some holding pens up there," Rachel said with some excitement. "Up in those hills somewhere. Maybe they're working some deals in Stonetown."

"That's not exactly a friendly place," Kevin muttered darkly.

"Do you have any law handy?" asked Slocum, aware of Rachel's puzzled glance but wanting to see what reaction he would get from the two men.

Neither of them seemed very happy. The old man sighed and looked sadly down at the fork in his hand, not seeing it, as if his mind were filled with memories of a better time. As if, thought Slocum, he was just as disappointed in his old friend as Rachel was.

The effect on Kevin was sharper. He almost winced at the idea of calling in the sheriff, Henry Wingfield. "I guess it wouldn't hurt to take a ride over that way," he said without enthusiasm. "Not that I think we'll find anything."

"Not even in Stonetown?" said Slocum.

"The boys can handle it if we do," Kevin said, giving him an unpleasant look.

"But it wouldn't hurt to have more help," Rachel said suddenly. "I mean, I was thinking . . . Mr. Slocum seems like he might be pretty capable if it came to a fight." She was staring at her hands now, rubbing them together, and she didn't see her father grinning at Slocum. "That is, if he was willing to hire on for a while . . ."

"Sorry, daughter," said Foley Anderson, still grinning, "but I don't think Mr. Slocum plans to stay in one place that long."

"Maybe it won't *take* that long," Slocum said.

"Oh, would you!" said Rachel, her face brightening in a way that made Slocum's heart beat a little faster.

The old man simply stared, forgetting to close his mouth.

Kevin Anderson was also staring, but with a hooded look of dark animosity that gave Slocum a chill, even in the warmth of the kitchen.

The bunkhouse was a lot bigger than the kitchen, but it was heated by a much smaller stove, which sat forlornly in a far corner. All eight of the ranch hands were huddled around the stove, watching Slocum as he came through the door into a sudden silence. He nodded briefly at the men as he headed for an empty bed, eyeing it longingly as he tossed his bedroll down and his bag beside it. The Henry he leaned gently against the wall, aware that the vaqueros were following every move. He squinted toward the stove, trying to read their expressions through the smoky haze. Mostly it was obvious that no one was trying to make him feel welcome.

"It doesn't look like they're working you boys hard enough," Slocum said cordially. "Either that, or you've found a substitute for sleep."

"Roundup's over," said one of the cowboys. "Tomorrow we sleep in and take it easy."

Slocum sighed deeply and reached into his bag for a small wooden case and a Colt Navy revolver that matched the one on his hip. "Afraid not," he said simply.

"I knew it!" said one of the hands, a chunky-looking Mexican with a heavy, drooping mustache. "It's those damn rustlers, ain't it?"

Slocum nodded. "Mr. Anderson asked me to tell you. We ride with first light."

"God *damn* it," the Mexican said irritably, looking around at the men by the stove. "Didn't I tell you?"

There was a general murmur of disgruntled voices. Slocum pulled an empty chair into the circle by the fire and sat down. He had a chance to let his eyes wander while the men griped to each other, and within a few seconds he had a general feel for the group. Exactly half of the cowboys had come up from south of the border, which was just thirty miles away, and the big man with the bandit mustache was the only who held Slocum's attention. He seemed to be leading the discussion. Slocum also took note of a skinny Mexican who was staring moodily toward the stove while the others talked excitedly about the day to come.

Two of the four remaining hands, the gringos, looked like nothing more than dull, slow-witted laborers. A third had the soft skin and faintly elegant manner of a newly arrived Easterner, and he was staring at the yammering Mexicans as if they were creatures from across the ocean.

Slocum's gaze finally came to rest on a solidly built red-haired man who was lounging farther back in the shadows, slightly apart from the others, and whose eyes met Slocum's directly. Slocum realized that the man had been giving him the same close scrutiny that he had been giving everyone else, which naturally aroused Slocum's interest. Neither man looked away. Instead they measured each other openly, recognizing something they shared but which they would have had a hard time giving a name to. *This is someone I'd better keep an eye on,* Slocum told himself, knowing that the red-haired man was probably telling himself the same thing.

It was Slocum who finally broke the spell, lowering his eyes to make a deliberate show of opening the small wooden case on his right knee. A couple of the cowboys glanced over at him, then lost interest when they saw what he was doing. They went on talking as Slocum began to pry the lead balls out of the cylinder of each Colt, dropping them one by one into the open cover of the case. He also scooped out the black powder beneath the slugs and carefully cleaned each chamber. Then he popped out the tiny caps that would have exploded with the impact of the hammer.

"You must be expecting trouble tomorrow," the red-haired man said in a low, easy tone.

Slocum looked up, pondering the twinkle in those solemn grey eyes. "I never expect it," he said with a little smile of his own, "but I always try to be ready for it. Too many good men have died snapping at bad caps or damp powder."

The red-haired man nodded. Slocum reached for the small tin powderhorn in his case, upending it over each chamber and filling them with carefully measured amounts of power.

"Or maybe I'm missing the point," Slocum said suddenly. *"Should* I be expecting trouble tomorrow?"

The red-haired man shrugged. "The bastards have never left a trace before," he said. "I don't see why tomorrow should be any different."

"Not having much luck, then."

"You can say that twice."

The Mexicans had stopped jabbering and now the fat one with the mustache made a sound of disgust. "They always find a way to do their work where we are not," he told Slocum. "By the time we discover what has happened, they have vanished with no trail remaining. Only once was there a trail, but it vanished, too, before we had followed very far. These bandits are like ghosts, *señor*."

Slocum nodded thoughtfully, holding one of the lead balls up to the candlelight and turning it in his fingers. "That's about what they were saying inside," he murmured. "It kind of made me wonder." Satisfied that there were no nicks or dents in the ball, Slocum pressed it into a chamber with his thumb, turned the cylinder until the chamber was underneath the ramrod, then pulled down the lever that packed the ball up tight against the powder, and the powder against the backside of the cap. He held another ball up against the light and asked, "How long has this been going on?"

The ranch hands looked at each other. "Almost a year?" said the Mexican. "We started losing cattle sometime last fall."

"And always the same pattern?" Slocum asked, inspecting a third ball. "The theft isn't discovered for a few days because you boys are working somewhere else on the ranch?"

"That's the way it's been so far," said the Mexican.

"It's only an accident that things are any different this time," Slocum said. "If I hadn't come along to find that calf—and if Miss Rachel hadn't guessed at what it meant—you'd still be sleeping late tomorrow."

"You speak the truth, *señor*."

"So it kind of makes you wonder, doesn't it."

"Wonder what?" said the red-haired man, his voice now an ominous rumble.

"Well, for one thing," Slocum said, returning the man's level stare, "it makes me wonder why a man who seems half bright would even have to ask that question."

"Then again, a half-bright man ought to know the answer to some of his own questions," the red-haired man said calmly.

Slocum began recharging the second Colt, noticing that most of the vaqueros were watching this exchange with confusion; only a couple wore looks of anticipation. "You want me to say it straight out, then?" he asked.

"It would be best. Just to avoid any misunderstandings."

"I don't see what there is to misunderstand," Slocum said, turning a ball in his fingers. "It seems pretty obvious that the rustlers have an inside contact. That one of you—at the least—is tipping them off."

Now even the slowest of the hands were giving Slocum evil looks. The Mexican with the mustache started to say something, but deferred to the red-haired man, who only sighed and shook his head. "Maybe I was wrong about you being half bright," he told Slocum. "It doesn't make good sense to waltz in here and right away start accusing a bunch of unhappy, worn-out, pissed-off hands who consider themselves loyal to the brand."

"I'm not accusing *all* of you. But it does seem to me you're taking it mighty personal."

Another sigh, and the red-haried man slowly got to his feet. "You're not learning any too quick," he said. "Maybe you need a lesson or two in good manners."

There was a chorus of chair legs scraping over the rough wooden floor as the other cowboys also got out of their chairs, backing off a little to make room. Slocum watched them form a natural ring as he carefully tamped home the last of the charges. Then he replaced his tools in the small wooden case, closed it, and carried the case and both Colts over to the bed. There was a tense silence in the room as the men waited, ready to jump in if Slocum tried anything with the Colts. Once he had placed the revolvers safely on the bed the cowboys moved back a little farther, while the red-haired man advanced toward Slocum with his hands clenched down at his sides.

"This isn't really necessary, is it?" Slocum said innocently, knowing perfectly well that he and the red-haired

man would have to test each other. It was almost pre-
ordained from the moment their eyes met. "If you're not
a thief, then there's no offense."

"You're accusing the men I ride with," said the man.
"That's offense enough for me."

Slocum shrugged, and swung suddenly from the hip.
He was aiming for the big man's jaw with a blow that
could have ended the fight right there, but his fist never
connected. The red-haired man was just as fast as he
was big, and maybe just as smart. Smart enough, at
least, to be expecting some kind of surprise. His left
arm swept up and deflected the punch, while his right
fist drove deep into Slocum's unprotected stomach. Slocum doubled over, gagging, and instantly felt another
crashing blow to his temple. He crumpled to the floor
and curled into something like a ball, trying to roll away
from the red-haired man, thinking for an instant that the
bastard must have three hands.

Slocum cursed himself for the worst mistake possible: underestimating his opponent. It could have been a
fatal mistake if this had been a fight for survival, where
you don't get a sporting chance to recover. Slocum had
sized up the red-haired man as the slow and lumbering
kind of fighter, but he was changing all his assumptions
as he came off the floor. And a good thing, too. The son
of a bitch was right there, ready and waiting.

Slocum came up with his guard in place, shaking his
head to clear it a little but still alert enough to prevent
any more serious damage. For a couple of minutes the
two men went around like boxers, slipping each other's
punches or trying to take them on their shoulders and
arms. Their labored breathing was the only sound in the
room, apart from the occasional grunt or the slap of
knuckles against flesh. There had been a cheer or two
when the red-haired man knocked Slocum to the floor,
but after that the other hands had mostly been content to
watch in silence. Slocum tried bearing down, throwing

a flurry of punches as he advanced, but the red-haired man simply gave ground without getting excited, grazing Slocum's jaw when he found an opening.

"You're just as stubborn as you look," Slocum told him, "but a hell of a lot faster."

The other man grinned tightly. "And you ain't exactly an easy man to keep on the ground."

"Well, I don't see it very often."

Slocum tried a left jab and then another right, another powerful swing designed to end the fight, but the red-haired man took the blow on his shoulder and went for Slocum's gut again, exposing his neck in the process. Slocum was already rolling off to the side, half expecting this repetition of strategy. He let the big fist breeze by in front of him this time. Slocum also took a short jab at at the man's neck, which snapped his head back and sent him reeling. Slocum came around with a wide swing into the red-haired man's stomach, following with another left to the jaw and a right to the side of the head. The red-haired man struggled to keep his arms up, but Slocum hit him twice more and then stepped back to watch him fold to the floor.

The red-haired man rolled onto his hands and knees after a moment, trying to get up, but instead he fell onto his side and felt his jaw with one hand, looking dazedly up at Slocum. "I hope I taught you a lesson," he said thickly.

Slocum laughed out loud, taking a liking to the man in that moment. "Yeah, in a way you did," he said, extending a hand to help him up. "I was wondering what kind of men I'd be riding with tomorrow. Now I know."

The red-haired man let Slocum pull him to his feet. "I guess we know a little more about you, too."

"Well, now that we're all acquainted," Slocum said dryly, "why don't I break a flask of whiskey out of my bag."

"For medicinal purposes?" said the red-haired man, still stroking his jaw.

"Of course," Slocum said with a grin. "Good for all the aches and pains of a hard life."

7

Breakfast the next morning was a sullen time for the hired hands of the Rancho de Plata. The sky had just begun to turn grey when they shuffled silently into the kitchen after less than five hours' sleep, trying not to show how stiff and sore they were after five days of cutting, roping, and branding. Most of them chewed on their bacon and sipped at their coffee and went out to find their mounts without ever saying a word. It was enough to make Slocum feel a little gloomy himself.

It cheered him up to notice that he and the red-haired man appeared to be gravitating together, going from place to place more or less together by a kind of mutual understanding. Slocum figured that not only would it be pleasant to have a friendly face to talk to, but also to have someone he might be able to trust who could tell him more about what was happening at the Lazy K. The two men had talked a little longer the night before, swapping stories, and Slocum had learned that the other man's name was Mitchell Boyd, from South Texas. He had been prospecting in Montana during the War between the States, so he had taken no part in it, but he had gotten himself in a few scrapes with the Indians and he'd shot at rustlers now and then, after he decided that prospecting was too undignified and went back to pushing cattle. He told Slocum he had been working the Lazy K for two years, which was longer than he'd ever

stayed anywhere before. Slocum had briefly wondered
what the attraction was, and then forgot about it. He
figured out the answer the next morning after breakfast,
after they'd caught up their horses. Mitch Boyd glanced
over the saddle he'd just thrown onto his mustang and
whispered, "Oh, Lord, there she is."

Slocum looked up to see Rachel Anderson standing
in the front door of the adobe, watching the men get
ready, and his reaction was a lot like Boyd's. A hot,
prickly feeling ran along his skin when he saw her wild
red hair and her breasts straining the fabric of her shirt.
He also thought he saw a kind of misty sad look in her
eyes that tugged at his heart. He stopped working a
minute to stare at her, wanting to console her and to rip
off all her clothes at the same time. It seemed as if her
eyes were seeking him out, but he wasn't sure. Then he
realized that Boyd was watching him.

"Now, wouldn't it be just my luck," said Boyd.
"Here I've been waiting two years for a chance at that
girl, and some trail bum comes along to sweep her off
her feet."

Slocum had to look away. "Does your luck always
run that bad?" he said.

"Well, so far it ain't exactly been good."

"Then it can only get better, can't it?" Slocum was
able to look him in the eye again, now that he was about
to get closer to the truth. "Anyway, I'm just passing
through. I've hardly ever stopped in one place longer
than it takes to kick the dust off my boots and have a
good meal."

"Glad to hear it," said Boyd, showing a smile to take
the sting out of a remark that was sort of a compliment,
anyway. "I ain't so pretty or so rich that I don't have to
worry about competition."

"Seems to me two redheads would just naturally fall
all over each other," Slocum said with a smile. Then he
turned serious. "It also seems to me you'd have compe-

tition from every man in New Mexico, when it comes to a woman who looks like that."

Boyd's eyes lost their humor as he frowned over the top of his saddle. "It's the damnedest thing, Slocum, but she don't seem to have much use for men. They used to come around, sure, but she managed to discourage 'em, just like she done me. Most of 'em have given up, but I keep hopin' that if I stick around long enough, I'll figure her out."

Slocum grinned. "That's got to be the most optimistic thing I've ever heard a man say, Mitch. I just hope you don't get old and grey and die here, trying to do it."

"Naw," said the big man, shuffling his feet and grinning. "I'll give it up one of these days. Just as soon as I find another girl that looks like her."

Slocum sighed, and both men were sneaking another look at the woman when they saw her father appear in the doorway. She said something to him, and he appeared to answer with a stiff shake of his head. She talked some more, as if she were pleading with him, and he seemed to ignore her.

"She's probably wanting to come along," Boyd said with an amused smile.

"And the old man don't like the idea?" Slocum said, just to get Boyd's view of the situation.

"Of course not. This ain't no job for a woman."

Slocum nodded toward the house. "She seems to think different."

"Sure," Boyd said tolerantly. "She'd probably like to take over the ranch, too, once her father's gone. Hell, I might even feel the same way if my only other choice was all that cookin' and cleanin' and washin'. But her father has other ideas."

"They wouldn't by any chance be the same ideas you have, would they?"

Boyd laughed. "Well, now that you mention it." In the next instant his lips turned down as if he'd just tasted something sour. "Then again," he said, staring moodily toward the house, "I think I'd rather see the Lazy K in her hands than Kevin's."

Slocum followed Boyd's gaze and saw that Rachel's brother had now made his appearance in front of the 'dobe. Rachel appeared to be arguing with him and her father both. The old man was simply ignoring her now, stepping rigidly into the yard; Kevin shrugged his shoulders and then ambled after his father.

"You don't think the boy's up to it?" Slocum prompted.

"That kid is just about useless, Slocum."

"I have to admit, it didn't seem like he had his heart in it."

"The old man's trying every way he knows how to turn Kevin into a real cowman, but you're right—the kid don't give a shit. At least about cows."

"You mean there is something he cares about?"

Boyd thought about it. "Seems like there oughta be, don't it? He spends a lot of time goin' into Chandlerville, I know that, but don't ask me what he does there. Christ, the old man don't look so good today."

Slocum took a closer look and saw that the stiffness he had noticed earlier was more like an old man trying to hold himself together, trying to keep the lines of pain out of his face, which looked very pale in the early light. It was obvious from the way he walked that Foley Anderson's shattered knees were giving him plenty of trouble—and maybe something else. He took the reins to a big line-back dun from the Mexican with the mustache, who looked at the ground for a moment when the old man had to use his hands to put his boot into the stirrup. He pulled himself into the saddle easily enough —or so it looked. But then he sat there for a moment, recovering from the effort, and Slocum realized how hard he had worked to make it look easy.

"I've never seen him look this bad before," Boyd said softly.

"This isn't the first time, then?"

"He's getting old," Boyd said. "But now it seems to come in spells, like when he's worked too hard and too long."

Kevin Anderson and the vaqueros had all mounted up, but Foley Anderson was still sitting his horse and staring off into the distance beyond the house. His son was watching him with a puzzled expression. The old man's body seemed to sag a little, and then, very slowly, he turned his horse toward the waiting riders. His face had lost its stiffness. It was deeply furrowed now, as if the man had aged twenty years in as many seconds.

"I guess my son will have to run this little party," he said in a heavy tone of defeat. "I was wantin' to go with you, but I'd just be slowing you down, and I have to consider what's best for the ranch." He shook his head and looked at his men. "Don't ever get old if you can help it, boys. That's when you pay for all your sins."

A couple of the cowboys grinned nervously, but Slocum found himself feeling too sorry for the old man, who was slowly easing himself down from the saddle. "That must have been a hard thing to do," Slocum muttered.

"Especially for that stubborn old coot," said Boyd, with a sudden impatient scowl. "I mean, I'm sorry he had to embarrass himself that way, and I'm sorry he's feeling so poorly. But what I'm really sorry about is that now we're left to ride under that worthless kid of his. If we're not careful the bastard will get us all killed."

"Going up against three lowlife rustlers?"

"It ain't them snakes by themselves that worry me, it's the whole den of 'em back in the hills. Those thieves stick together."

"You're talking about Stonetown, I take it?"

Boyd gave him a sharp look. "You know the place?"

"Just from what the girl told me yesterday," Slocum said, nodding toward the house. Rachel Anderson had tried to help her father through the door, but he had shrugged her off irritably. Slocum felt a little less sorry for him, remembering the way he treated his daughter. Slocum faced the cowboy again, letting the trace of a smile turn up the corners of his lips. "Don't worry, Mitch, I don't have any personal experience of the place."

"I wasn't sayin' you did," Boyd said stiffly.

"But it crossed your mind—and I'd have to wonder about you if it didn't. I didn't exactly show up here with references, you know."

Boyd rubbed his jaw, grinning ruefully. "You got enough references as far as I'm concerned, Slocum. It looks like our leader ain't no happier than we are."

Kevin Anderson, who had been watching his father walk back into the house, turned back to the riders with a poorly disguised scowl darkening his features. He looked like a man carrying a heavy burden. "Let's go," he said mournfully, nudging his horse into a slow walk.

Slocum leaned over toward Boyd and whispered, "Inspirational, ain't he?"

The big redhead grinned back and said, "Yeah. He inspires you to keep a close eye on your own backside."

Kevin Anderson led the procession back to the mouth of the arroyo and Slocum showed him the boulder where the rustlers had made their stand. The sun was already so hot at mid-morning that heat waves shimmered off the boulder in the distance, but there was still a little shade behind it. The riders rested there, taking off their hats and wiping their heads and tilting up their canteens while Slocum, Boyd, and Kevin Anderson studied the ground. Slocum picked up two or three large brass shell casings and turned them over in his hand.

"It's a good thing they were just trying to discourage us," he said. "I'd hate to get hit with the slugs that came out of these things."

"Take a look at this," said Boyd. He was farther along the face of the rock, kneeling over a dark patch in the ground. "I think they spilled some water. Enough to make a little bit of mud, anyway. And take a look at the print they left."

Slocum studied the print carefully—the only one behind the boulder that was clearly defined. There were plenty of scuff marks in the dirt, but the desert surface was so hard-baked that no impressions were left. Something had either hit it hard enough to crumble some of the dirt, or else it stayed the way it was, like a crust. But the little patch of mud had taken a perfect cast of a man's boot.

"Kind of a small fella," Boyd mused.

"None of 'em was exactly huge," Slocum said, "but I think I remember the one that might have left this print. He was riding a little Appaloosa, and I remember thinking that even the Appaloosa looked too big for him."

"You had a good look at him?" asked Kevin.

"As good as I could at three hundred yards, with him shooting at me."

"You wouldn't recognize him, then."

Slocum looked at the boy, trying to think of a civil reply.

"Well, you can sure recognize that boot," Boyd said, his voice showing some excitement. "All you have to do is find an Appaloosa with a rider who's got a long split in his heel."

"That's all?" said Slocum.

The red-haired man grinned up at him. "It's a hell of a lot more'n we've had all year. It could be a start of some kind."

"Any idea where they'd take the cows from here?" Slocum asked Kevin.

The young rancher shook his head and gazed up the arroyo with a weary frown. "I guess we might as well see if they left a trail."

Slocum and Boyd looked at each other as Kevin headed for his horse, then Boyd glanced up at the rim of the canyon. "Mr. Anderson," he said.

Kevin stopped and turned back, waiting.

"Were we gonna just ride up the canyon?" said Boyd.

"If that's where the trail leads."

"I mean . . . I'd be glad to take one of the ridges, just to make sure we don't get jumped."

"Those bandits must be miles away," Kevin snapped.

"They still have to hole up somewhere," Slocum suggested. "At least long enough to change the brands. They might have found a natural holding pen right up here somewhere."

Kevin Anderson sighed deeply, looking up the arroyo again before he glanced from Slocum to Boyd. "I need you two down here," he finally said. "I'll send Chavez and Guttierez."

These turned out to be the skinny Mexican who'd been staring into the fire in the stove, and the heavy one with the drooping mustache. Kevin gave them his orders, then followed the skinny one back to his horse and had another word or two with him. The rest of the men waited until the two outriders had picked their way up the sides of the canyon and reappeared on the rimrock about half a mile ahead, waving their hats. Then Kevin made a little half-hearted motion with his arm and the Lazy K riders moved out. Slocum and Boyd fell back to bring up the rear, keeping an eye on the ridges.

The hours went by and the sun eased up toward the middle of the sky, burning straight down into the canyon and baking the rocks so that Slocum could feel the heat reflecting at him from all sides. There was no breeze in the canyon to offer relief, or to blow away the dust being raised by Kevin and the five other vaqueros ahead of them. Slocum and Boyd lagged farther and farther behind, giving the dust a chance to thin out a little so they would have some air to breathe and so they could more or less see the ridges along the arroyo.

"I suspect we ought to pay a little more attention to the right side than the left," Boyd told Slocum sometime after noon. "That skinny little Mexican ain't never seemed quite right to me."

"Was that Guttierez or Chavez?"

"Guttierez. Chavez just looks like a bandit, with that big mustache, but he does all right in a scrape."

"I wonder why Kevin chose the skinny one for such an important job."

Boyd made a sound of disgust. "Maybe those worthless types just like to look out for each other. All I can say is—"

Slocum glanced back when Boyd stopped in the middle of his sentence, and saw the redhead staring up the canyon. In that moment he heard a volley of rifle fire, just as Boyd spurred his mount past Slocum, who knew instantly that Boyd had seen the puffs of smoke from the rifles before the sounds of the firing could reach them. Slocum was spurring his own horse instinctively now, all his reactions a split second behind Boyd's, but in that short time he was able to see and understand something that Boyd was missing.

"Stop!" he shouted to the cowboy, trying desperately to catch up. "They're killing the horses."

He saw Boyd look up and almost immediately rear back in the saddle, pulling on the reins as soon as he understood the danger. A hundred yards up the canyon the Lazy K horses were reeling in confusion and panic. They were kicking up enough dust to obscure some of what was happening, but Boyd and Slocum could see at least two horses down and kicking. They could also hear the animals' screams of fright and agony. Slocum came alongside and gained a little when Boyd yanked on his reins, the two of them trying to cut a tight circle in the narrow canyon. Their mounts sidled together so that their legs and saddles were knocking against each other. Slocum glanced over his shoulder and saw more horses down amid the billowing clouds of dust. He also saw little spouts of dust coming toward them down the arroyo, and knew that some of the shooters on the ridge were trying to get their range. He was frantically lashing his pony's flanks when he felt a solid, thudding vibration through the skirt of his saddle.

"God damn it to hell," Slocum muttered hopelessly.

He was setting himself to jump free when his pony shuddered and stumbled, pitching itself right into Boyd's path. Both horses and both riders went tumbling end over end, a terrible flurry of arms and legs and flying hooves smashing the hard-baked earth to the steady beat of distant gunfire.

For just a moment it seemed as if time had slowed to a gentle ooze for Slocum, as if he could step easily and gracefully out of his predicament, and then time stopped altogether when something crashed against his temple. He felt his body hit the ground, and vaguely he heard the screaming of another horse, closer and yet far away. He still heard the rifles on the ridge which spoke of danger, and he considered trying to get up, but it was just too much effort. Later it seemed like there were two more shots, closer by and evenly spaced. It might have been about that time that one of the horses stopped screaming, and it wasn't too much later that Slocum gave up and drifted away.

8

It was the sound of a shot that woke Slocum up again, or at least that was the first sound he was aware of after he came back to consciousness. His eyes moved behind closed lids and instantly there was a sharp searing pain on the side of his head, followed by a dull hammering ache when he clenched his jaw. He thought about moving, but he figured there wasn't much point. He wasn't dead yet, and whoever was doing the shooting had had plenty of opportunity. He started realizing how silent it was, and he noticed that the sun wasn't burning so hot against his skin. He had probably been out for a while, then. The crack of another rifle shot came drifting down from the ridge, and Slocum started to get mildly curious about what had happened. His first major project was opening his eyes. After staring at the white-hot sky for a minute or two, he carefully twisted his head around and let his eyes come to rest on Mitch Boyd, who was propped up on an elbow behind his dead horse. Boyd grinned when he saw Slocum.

"You were smart, getting knocked on the head like that," he said. "The rest of us have just had to sit out here and be miserable all afternoon."

"What the hell hit me?" Slocum asked.

"One of my pony's hooves, I s'pose. Maybe that's what broke his leg." He tried to say it lightly but he sounded grim. "I sure hated to put him down."

73

Slocum remembered the evenly spaced shots that had come from close by. "You do the same for mine?" he asked.

Boyd nodded. "Yours got hit in the gut. The bastards got two horses for the price of one bullet."

"They'll pay a higher price than that," Slocum said bitterly, a cold rage seeping through him to take his mind off the pain. "They'll be sorry they ever saw New Mexico." He twisted around and struggled to his knees, trying to look up the canyon. "Anyway, thanks for putting my pony out of his misery. How are the others?"

"The other horses?" Boyd said with sour humor. "Every one of 'em is down. The men seem to be all in one piece."

"That's something, anyway. We still pinned down?"

"I ain't sittin' out in the sun like this just for my health. Every time someone tries to make a move, a slug lands somewhere close by to give him second thoughts."

"But no one's hit yet?"

"Not that I know of."

Slocum frowned at that. He'd been wandering around for quite a few years and so far he'd never met up with such a well-mannered bunch of thieves. The boys from the Rancho de Plata would be sure to hang them for rustling anyway if they ever caught up with them, so Slocum couldn't understand what the bandits thought they might gain by being so polite. Then he got to thinking about the sheriff Rachel had mentioned.

"Say, Mitch," Slocum said, "how much farther do you figure it is to this Stonetown I keep hearing about?"

Boyd squinted up the canyon, thinking. "No more than five miles, I'd say. Why?"

"And what about . . . what's the sheriff's name hereabouts?"

"Henry Wingfield. What've you got in mind?"

"Wingfield, that was it. Rachel gave me the idea he

wasn't having too much luck with this rustling."

"Maybe he ain't the man he used to be, Slocum."

"That could go a lot of ways. You think maybe he lets Stonetown stay in business, as long as nothing too serious happens to the locals?"

"Damn," said Boyd, "I'd hate to think it."

"Why else would our friends on the ridge be so nice to us?"

"You got me. Although I don't exactly feel friendly about walking twenty or thirty miles back to the ranch."

"It'll be dark and cool, at least."

Boyd looked up at the sky, shading his eyes with his hand. "Sundown can't be too far. Maybe that's when they'll let us go."

The sky dimmed slowly into darker shades of blue and the silence seemed to get deeper, broken only once or twice by the buzzing of a fly. Slocum could feel a chill come to the air, although the rocks were still radiating the warmth they'd soaked up from the sun.

"I'm beginning to think we're alone," Slocum said after another hour had gone by. He climbed slowly to his feet, putting his hand to his head when the canyon started to spin around him. He felt caked blood in front of his ear, and a soft pulpiness beneath his fingers, but nothing that would indicate a broken skull. He tried a few steps, and when nothing happened Boyd got up from behind his dead horse and joined him. But Slocum didn't continue on toward the other group of men. Instead he turned on his heel and knelt beside his own dead horse, stripping it of the saddle and the rest of the rigging. Then he headed up the canyon with the saddle over his shoulder and the reins dragging from his left hand, Boyd following at his side with a curious frown.

Kevin Anderson and the vaqueros had taken courage from Slocum's approach and were standing now, still with an occasional nervous glance toward the ridge. A couple of them threw rifles to their shoulders when a rider suddenly appeared above them, lowering them when they recognized the Mexican with the mustache, Chavez, just in time. They were surprised because he was supposed to have been on the opposite side, but when he started down they saw that the skinny Mexican was riding limply behind him. Their heavily loaded horse slid and slipped as carefully as it could down the side of the arroyo, arriving just about the time Slocum and Boyd walked up.

"I could never get a clear shot," Chavez was explaining apologetically to Kevin. "It was too far and their cover was too good. I worked back down and came up the other side, but there were so many..."

"You did the right thing," Kevin Anderson said.

"If they'd been shooting to kill," Chavez began, looking distressed.

Anderson raised his hand. "Don't worry, Tibo. It was bad luck all around."

"Yes, sir," said Chavez. "I found Jesus after they had gone, tied to a rock. He claims they struck him from behind."

"*Sí,*" said the other man on the horse. "I'm hit on head, an' that ees last thing I know."

The skinny Mexican had a lump behind his ear and a trail of dried blood leading down his neck and under his collar. Guttierez looked the way Slocum felt, except that Slocum was still suspicious of the vaquero who had let the party get bushwhacked. Anyone could take a lump on the head to make a story look good.

Kevin Anderson looked around at his men with a solemn and weary expression of defeat. "Maybe we should just be thankful for the one horse we got left," he said sadly. "It'll be a long walk back."

"Stonetown's a lot closer," Slocum said.

Anderson looked at him as if he were crazy. "Where the hell do you think those bushwhackers came from, Slocum?"

"That's my point, Kevin. Are you just gonna let the men who killed all your animals—not to mention the ones they've been stealing—you're planning to let them walk away?"

"Don't worry, we'll find 'em."

Slocum struggled to keep the disgust out of his voice. "They're up there *now*, Kevin. This is no time to give up. I'm sure your father wouldn't quit if he was here."

The young rancher reared back, his eyes suddenly burning with more emotion than Slocum had ever seen him display. "I don't care what *he* would have done," Kevin said through clenched teeth. "He put me in charge, so it's my responsibility."

"Do you want to inherit an empty ranch?" Slocum said, surprised and puzzled. "That's what it'll be if you don't go after those bandits while you have the chance."

"Don't tell me my business," Kevin raged. "I won't have it! Especially not from some goddamned over-dressed tramp who doesn't have any idea what he's talking about."

Slocum's puzzled feeling disappeared in a cold wave of anger that blanked out everything else. He had let the saddle drop from his hand but he didn't realize how he was looking at Kevin until Boyd stepped up to face him, taking a light grip on his gun arm. "He's just a dumb kid," murmured the cowboy. "Growed up in years, maybe, but that's all."

"How did he get to live so long, with a mouth like that?"

Boyd shrugged and a few seconds later Slocum began to breathe a little easier. "If this was five years ago," Slocum told the rancher in a deadly tone, "you'd be laid out right now with a bullet in your gut. You're lucky I finally figured out who's worth killin' and who ain't." With that he bent to pick up his saddle again and started walking up the canyon.

"Where are you going?" called Boyd.

"To find out who killed my horse," Slocum said over his shoulder.

"But Stonetown is miles away!" said Kevin Anderson.

Slocum laughed bitterly. "I'll be there a lot quicker than you get home," he called back without stopping.

"Except you'll still be without a horse."

"Not for long."

"Stop this!" Kevin yelled. "I order you to come back. I can't take the responsibility."

Slocum spun on his heel, giving the rancher a long stare. "Do you really think I still work for you?" he sneered.

"If you continue, Slocum, you'd better make sure you never again set foot on Lazy K land. I'll see that you're shot for trespassing."

"You don't have the balls to do that," said Slocum, "and you never will." He stared at Anderson a moment longer and then, with slow, deliberate insolence, turned his back again and started walking.

"Wait!" said Boyd. "Let me get the gear off my horse."

Slocum and Boyd hid their traps under some brush and slipped into Stonetown well after dark, but before the half moon had risen above the mountains. All they saw were the hulking shadows of twelve or thirteen rough adobe buildings—Stonetown was dozens of miles from the nearest forest—only four or five of which were showing light. The 'dobes were scattered in a shallow basin that formed a natural fortress, with no pattern or streets that Slocum could see. Boyd said Stonetown had been a mining town at one time, serving a few silver workings up and down the arroyos, which had quickly played out. He said no one knew whether the town's name referred to the stone that the miners had to cut through to get their silver, or to being stony broke when the silver proved hard to find. One or two prospectors were said to be still roaming the mountains, refusing to quit, but they had to get along with the rustlers, thieves, and other hardcases who were apparently finding Stonetown to be an ideal refuge.

"God damn," Boyd whispered in Slocum's ear as the two men padded between the buildings. "I haven't had this much fun in a dog's age."

"I'm glad," Slocum whispered back. "Because I don't think you have a job any more."

"There's always jobs."

"Maybe, but there's only one Rachel."

"Yeah, well . . ." Boyd sighed, and Slocum knew the thought hit him harder than he wanted to admit. "I guess it's just a fool that don't know when to give up on a woman, anyway."

Slocum figured it was time to give up arguing with Boyd. The man had insisted on coming along, no matter how many objections Slocum raised, right from the beginning. Kevin Anderson hadn't threatened Boyd the way he'd threatened Slocum, but he'd been angered by the switch in loyalties and the loss of a good hand. Slocum had followed along with Boyd while he retrieved his saddle and rifle from under his dead horse, trying hard to talk him out of coming along.

"I don't need you," Slocum had said.

"Sure you do," the redhead had answered, offering a friendly wink as he unbuckled the cinch strap. "I'll watch your back while you watch the front."

"What if Anderson fires you?"

"Then I won't have to follow his orders to shoot you as a trespasser." Boyd glanced down at the mustang as he worked to free the saddle, and his friendly banter had suddenly given way to a hard glare. "Those bastards killed my horse too, Slocum. But, worse than that, they've been making monkeys of us all winter."

"Seems to bother you more than it does the guy who *owns* the cattle," Slocum had remarked mildly.

"Yeah," Boyd had said, yanking his gear free and throwing it over his shoulder. "So let's get the hell out of here."

Now they were walking quietly through the middle of the outlaw town, unseen and unchallenged for the moment, drawn toward the shouts and laughter spilling out of the most brightly lit adobe. Slocum assumed it was the Stonetown equivalent of saloon and whorehouse—if they could find any girls willing to stay up here—and he stopped to study it from the shadows beside a dark house on the other side of an open space that looked something like a town plaza, but without a gazebo.

A couple of the buildings that glimmered faintly in what little light there was might have been stores at one time—maybe they still were, for that matter. None of the 'dobes had been stuccoed, as if the men who built them had realized early on that they would not be staying. They had simply mixed their mud and straw and then stacked the bricks when they were dry, leaving them exposed to the occasional rain so that they had begun to melt together. On the east side there were two smaller adobes that might have been living quarters, showing no light, while one large building dominated the west side. It was the only frame structure there, made of rough wooden planks, and Slocum noticed a tall swinging door, marking it as a probable livery barn. The lanternlight didn't reach much farther than the square, but the longer Slocum stared beyond the livery the more he convinced himself he could see the poles of a corral behind it. He touched Boyd's arm and then pointed in that direction.

"I bet that's where we'll find some horses," he said quietly, beneath a sudden burst of noise from the saloon. "When the time comes."

"I don't suppose you've come up with any kind of plan yet."

"Just to walk in and see what happens."

"Like knockin' down a hornets' nest to see what comes out," Boyd grunted.

"You sure got a gift for words," Slocum said with a grin. "I hope you show equal talents when it comes to a fight."

"Just lead me to the hornets' nest."

"Sure," said Slocum. He stepped out of the shadows without another word and started walking toward the saloon.

"Oh, shit," muttered Boyd.

He followed Slocum into the saloon and stopped instinctively just inside the open door, back to the wall, peering carefully through the dim lanternlight thick with smoke. Slocum ambled up to the bar, which was just two long planks sagging between a couple of empty whiskey kegs. Boyd counted eight men in the room, one of whom had a frail-looking blonde sitting on his lap. They had more or less stopped talking when Slocum came through the door, surprised first of all by the appearance of two strangers whom none of them recognized—confirmed by a few glances among themselves and a few shoulders shrugged—and second of all by how sudden the appearance was, with no sound of horses to announce it. One of the customers immediately slipped out through the back door, before Boyd could do anything about it.

Slocum was buying a bottle. The bartender plunked two glasses down on the boards and Slocum flipped him a double eagle. Boyd was a little curious about where the coin came from, and so was everyone else in the saloon. They solemnly watched the transaction while Boyd watched them. When it seemed that no one was about to pull a gun, he went to sit with Slocum at a rough table against the wall opposite the bar.

"I can see you're a man that likes taking chances," Boyd mumbled as he sat down.

"This is a picnic compared to some spots we were in with Quantrill."

It was something Slocum didn't normally talk about, and he didn't want it to seem that he was boasting, but he thought the information might give Boyd a little confidence. It seemed to work, as far as he could tell. Boyd lifted an eyebrow and his glass and tossed back a shot of whiskey, then leaned his shoulder against the wall, breathing easier, but wearing a sour expression.

"Now I know what they do with all the cow piss off the Lazy K," he said.

"Do you really think the whiskey tastes that *good?*" said Slocum. "There's gotta be gunpowder and snake venom in here for the real flavor."

"Might be just as well to get used to it. Gunpowder is something we're apt to be getting plenty of."

"All the more reason to enjoy our liquor while we're in good company," Slocum said with an easy smile around the room. "I don't see any sunburned necks in here, do you? It don't look like any of these gents spent the day out on the rim of a canyon."

"No, but you can bet they've heard of it, and they know the ones that did it. That runt that took off when you came in is probably on his way to tell them right now."

"But who knows how far he'll have to go?" Slocum said casually. "Besides, I thought we wanted to meet up with those boys."

"On our terms, not theirs. Christ, now here comes the girl."

Slocum looked up to see the little blonde advancing on him with an intent, hungry look in her gaunt and hollow face. She had seemed bored and sleepy when he first noticed her, but that was before she'd seen him getting change for the twenty-dollar gold piece. Behind

her, the man whose lap she'd been sitting on was struggling to his feet. He had the unsteady look of a man
who had been drinking for a long time, and the mean
look of a man whose temper only gets worse with the
addition of rotgut. There was a cruel glint behind the
puzzlement in his black eyes.

"Julie?" he said. "Where you goin', Julie?"

"Just bein' hospitable," she said to the man, while
she smiled at Slocum.

"You get back here, Julie. That cowpoke don't need
no hospitality."

"Oh, sure he does." She gave the big man a saucy
flip of her short blond hair, still staring at Slocum with
what he figured was supposed to be a provocative and
inviting look. It made him think of the way a cat
watches a mouse. "You shush now, Frank," said the
girl. "I'll be around by 'n' by."

"Julie," said the man named Frank. He just said her
name, standing there and watching her, but the way he
said it was clearly a warning, backed up by the way his
hands dangled near a pair of pistols on his hips. Slocum
sighed, knowing from long experience how the rest of
the scene was likely to go. He also knew he could end it
now, and looking at Julie, he was tempted to. She
wasn't but a few inches over five feet, and she didn't
have any curves to brag about. But he decided there
were reasons to let it continue.

He realized that the girl was making a decision of her
own. She had heard the warning in the big man's voice,
and she knew he'd gone too far to back down without
making a fool of himself in front of everyone else in the
saloon. The girl had stopped in the middle of the small
room, glancing from Frank to Slocum and back again,
as if she were weighing one man against the other and
making careful calculations.

Mitchell Boyd leaned across the table and put his
mouth close to Slocum's ear. "No need to get involved

in this," he said in a low, nervous tone. "Don't get yourself killed just because the little bitch is bored."

Slocum nodded almost imperceptibly, carefully watching the girl as he made his own calculations.

The blonde's moment of indecision had passed. "Well, now, no wonder you're jealous," she said to the cruel-eyed man, her voice quavering a little. "The stranger is a lot better lookin' than you are, an' he's also got a lot more money." Slocum winced as the blonde sidled over and draped her arm around his neck. "You want to spend some of it on me?" she purred, rubbing her lean little body against Slocum. "I got me a place o' my own out back, mister, and I could show you a—"

The girl's head suddenly jerked back, a look of terror on her face. Slocum saw that the man named Frank had come up behind her and grabbed a handful of her short blond hair. He whipped his arm around and then let go, which sent her crashing into a table and some chairs halfway across the room. He leaped after her and before she could move he was swiping at her face with the back of his hand. "I guess you'll listen to me!" he hissed down at her, breathing through his teeth.

"Not for long," Slocum said, pushing his chair back. "Because you'll be dead."

The black-eyed man whirled around, palming his guns while Slocum's chair was still scraping along the dirt floor. He was fast and deadly, even with the whiskey, and he probably figured on catching Slocum in an awkward moment. Boyd was so surprised and alarmed that he went for his own gun, but before it was even out of its holster there was an explosion from the other side of the table. Boyd watched the bandit's body jerk, and then jerk again with the sound of a second shot as he was still trying to bring up his pistols. The bandit stayed on his feet a moment longer, his body swaying and a splotch of blood appearing on the front of his shirt, and then he pitched forward onto his face.

Boyd had his own gun out now and he was keeping an eye on the other customers, but it didn't seem to be necessary. They sat for a moment in shocked silence, staring down at the body, and then they looked at Slocum with anger, hatred, respect, and a little fear.

"Did you see it?" someone whispered near the back of the room. "Sitting down, *with his hand on the chair*. Nothing like I ever seen before."

Boyd was wishing he had seen it. If he'd known how fast Slocum was he wouldn't have been worried about watching the bandit, and he could have seen a true gunhand in action. Then it occurred to him that he would probably get plenty of other chances if they kept going after the rustlers. For some reason the thought didn't cheer him up very much.

The blonde had gotten to her feet and now she was staring down at the dead man, rubbing her jaw where he had hit her only a few seconds before. "Did you have to kill him?" she asked Slocum, her voice a breathless whisper.

"Probably not," Slocum said casually. "But it's exactly what you wanted. Now what was that you were telling me about a place out back?"

9

The girl's "place" was just a windowless room that might have been used as a pantry at one time, added on behind the saloon. Now there was almost nothing except a pile of bedding on the dirt floor and a small candle that sputtered poorly in the stale and sour-smelling air. Julie had led Slocum out through the back door of the saloon with a last nervous glance at the body on the floor and the six remaining men inside, but they were apparently still recovering from the shock of seeing Frank gunned down. Slocum didn't think much was going to happen for a few minutes, and that was all he needed. If he was wrong, then he felt he could rely on Mitch Boyd to keep an eye on the situation.

"I wish I could offer more of a place," said the girl as soon as they were in her room. She looked around forlornly, probably looking at the room the way she thought it would look through Slocum's eyes. "I've sure come a long way down since El Paso."

"Don't worry about it," Slocum said, a little too gruffly. "What I need from you won't take a lot of pretty furniture."

Julie turned to him and started unbuttoning his trousers, looking up at him from beneath her pale eyelashes. "You just want it in my mouth, you mean?"

Slocum shook his head. "Information. I want to know what you hear about rustling on the Rancho de Plata—or the Lazy K."

"Oh, no!" breathed the girl, sinking to her knees in front of Slocum and pulling out his shaft. "I mean, I don't know anything about it."

"Sure you do. The outlaws are among their own out here, so they can talk all they want about the jobs they pull. And you're right there to hear it . . . not to mention the bragging that goes on in this room."

"You're wrong," said the girl, in between kissing and licking him. "They never say anything in front of me." Slocum's cock was swollen hard despite his best efforts to keep his mind on business. She took it in her mouth, grasping and stroking its base with her hands, then let him slide out as if she was struck with a new idea. "They wouldn't *trust* me enough to talk."

"You're trying too hard to convince me," Slocum grunted. "You can go on with what you're doing, if you want—it feels pretty good—but it won't make any difference. You're going to tell me who's involved with the rustling."

"They'd kill me, mister! Please . . . don't make trouble."

"I'd say you made your own trouble when you threw in with this bunch."

The girl looked down at the floor, Slocum's manhood temporarily forgotten in her hand. "I didn't have no choice. One of 'em stole me out of El Paso an' brung me here, an' they never let me go." She raised her eyes, giving him a pleading look. "You think I'd come here by choice, mister? They don' even pay me, half the time. It was a lot softer life in El Paso."

Slocum didn't say anything for a moment. He was caught up in the girl's blue eyes, which were shining with dampness in the candlelight. Suddenly he shook himself and said, "It still won't work. I've already seen the way you can take care of yourself. You'll get by."

"What do you mean?" Julie almost whimpered.

"You didn't come to me for the money; you just

wanted to make trouble for Frank in there. He's the mean type, ain't he? Knocks you around when he feels like it?"

The girl didn't say anything, just knelt there holding onto Slocum, but her eyes were getting wider and there was a hint of fear in them.

"I thought so," said Slocum. "So a stranger walks in one night who looks like he might be a match for Frank. If he isn't, then the stranger gets killed and you just get a few bruises, which you're used to. But if the stranger's up to it, then you don't have to worry about Frank any more."

"Oh, please, mister, I didn't—"

"That's all right," Slocum said soothingly. "I went along with it and I didn't mind doing you a favor. I didn't like Frank's looks anyway. But now it's time for you to do me a favor."

"Anything! I mean, anything but talk."

"That's all I want from you."

"But I can make you feel good," the girl pleaded, nuzzling her cheek against him and stroking him some more. "Like you've never had it before."

Julie took him in her mouth again, smothering his member with attention from her tongue and lips and hands, and Slocum found it hard to get very mad at her. He knew he was going to have trouble making harsh, believable threats. He sighed and stroked her short blond hair with his fingers and said, "All right, let's get this part of it over with."

He was feeling so randy that he didn't think it would take very long. His time with Rachel the night before had given him plenty to think about all day, which was partly the reason for his low resistance now. Within a matter of seconds he had thrown his head back and was driving himself into the girl's mouth, only to realize that she was refusing to match his rhythm. He gripped her head between his hands, thrusting his hips forward with a great need, but she let her lips go slack around him. He was painfully close to satisfaction, yet it eluded him. Suddenly he heard a low, half-smothered giggle from deep in the girl's throat.

"You sure have a lot of tricks for a girl your age," Slocum snapped at her.

"But this is when it feels good, ain't it? For a man? Afterwards there won't be nothing but a deadness, and sometimes a sadness. Do you really want it to come so soon?"

"Yes and no," Slocum said with a little laugh.

"Do you want to lie down now?"

Slocum nodded. The girl finished unbuttoning his pants and pulled them down, all the while kissing and nuzzling his shaft. Slocum kicked the pants off and unbuckled his gunbelt when she reached down to lift her worn cotton dress over her head. Then she folded her legs out from beneath her and spread them wide apart as she lay back on the pile of bedding. Slocum knelt between her legs and leaned forward to cover her small body with his.

"Work it in nice and slow," she whispered, reaching down to guide him with her fingers. "Oh, yeah . . . that's it." And then, "You mean there's more?" She giggled again and wiggled beneath him. "You're gonna nail me right to the ground, stranger."

Slocum moved slowly at first, his shaft laboring in a tight grip, but the tightness only inflamed him that much sooner. Within a few seconds he was plunging wildly into the girl, who could no longer control his rhythm. She simply lay beneath him, pretending desire and making little sounds of encouragement in her throat, until Slocum went rigid and arched his back, feeling his release in her. Then he collapsed, catching his breath, holding most of his weight on his elbows.

"By the way," the girl said after a few seconds, "have you got a name?"

"John Slocum. Pleased to make your acquaintance."

The girl laughed, but not at his little joke. "Slocum?" she repeated. "Honey, your name don't fit you at all. There ain't nothing slow about the way *you* come!"

"I guess you outsmarted me again," Slocum said a few minutes later.

He had smiled at the girl's joke, enjoying it more than he'd enjoyed his own, and he let the silence stretch for a while. It wasn't too long before he'd slipped out of her, but he put on his pants and his gunbelt before he spoke again.

"Now you got me all lazy and feeling soft," he went on, "so it's hard for me to work up enough steam to try and scare you into talking." He looked into the girl's solemn eyes. "But the thing is, Julie, they'll know I was in here with you anyway. Have you thought about that? What are *they* gonna think when my partner and I go right on looking for those cattle thieves? We may not have much luck—hell, we may never come close—but what if we do? How do you think that will look?"

Fear had returned to the girl's face. Slocum could see her fine little nostrils quivering, and the rapid pulsing of an artery beneath a wisp of blond hair that hung down over the white skin of her temple.

"You see the problem?" Slocum prompted gently.

"Mister, please—can't you just get me out of here?"

"I've thought of that too, Julie, and I'd like to, but we have to make sure we can get ourselves out first. It may not be so easy. But the other thing I'm thinking is, it might be easier if we know what we're up against."

The girl was staring off into one of the dark corners of her windowless room, her eyes full of despair, but also intent on her thoughts.

"I'm sure you're smart enough to see my point," Slocum continued smoothly. "If we know how to take care of our problems, maybe we'll do it so fast that you'll be in the clear. Especially after we come back to take you away."

"That's real likely, ain't it?" the girl said bitterly.

"It's always possible," Slocum said with a grin, just before he looked serious again. "I can give you my word, Julie, which means something to me. But I suppose with your experience you wouldn't put much store in it. So it all comes back to the same old problem: they're likely to think you talked to me, whether you did or not."

"I understand that!" she snapped, still bitter. "I guess I can thank you for puttin' me between a rock and a goddamned hard place."

"Well, now," Slocum said easily, "I'd say you started the ball rolling yourself tonight, and you didn't particularly care how it might end up for me."

"You always got an answer, don't you?" The girl scowled at him and then looked into the dark corner again. "There's only four of 'em that I know of."

"Rustlers?"

"No, Mormon missionaries. Of course I mean rustlers! They been runnin' off stock for most of the year, and they keep bragging about how it's a risk-free operation."

"Because they have an inside man, right? Someone who lets them know what part of the range it's safest to raid?"

"Yeah," said the girl, turning to look more closely at Slocum. "How did you know that?"

"I'm not nearly as dumb as you seem to think I am. After all this time, half the Lazy K crew must suspect as much."

"Well, I hear they're planning to quit pretty soon. The thieves, I mean. This might have even been the last haul, or maybe the next one."

"That's interesting," Slocum said. "How many thieves do you know who know when it's time to quit?"

"The smart ones."

"Sure," Slocum said with a wry smile. "And when you get right down to it, how common is a smart thief?"

Julie smiled almost in spite of herself. "If I ever met one, I don't think I remember."

"Do you remember hearing where they pen these animals while they use a running iron?"

The girl shook her head.

"Or where they go after that?"

Another shake of the head. "There couldn't be much choice, though, could there? It's either over the border somewhere or else Mesilla. It don't seem like they'd trail a herd all the way down to El Paso."

"Who knows?" said Slocum. "There ain't nothing else about the situation that seems normal. Any idea who the inside man is?"

"I think the name was Guttierez."

Slocum nodded, his lips turning down in a scowl as he remembered the skinny little outrider who'd let them get bushwhacked. "I had a feeling about that bastard. His first name is Jesus?"

"It might be. I don't think I ever heard it."

"And the other three?" Slocum asked, remembering the three riders he and Rachel had seen the day before.

"No, I meant four men besides Guttierez."

"I only saw three yesterday."

Julie nodded. "They do all the work. The other one kind of stays in the shadows."

"But it's not Guttierez?"

"Oh, no, it's someone who just gives the orders. The three men who're actually making the raises, they just answer to this other one . . . whoever he is. They're only the hired help."

"What about a man named Tibo Chavez?" Slocum asked, thinking of the big Mexican with the bandit mustache who had ridden on the other ridge. "Have you heard of him?"

"Nope. No one named Chavez."

Slocum thought about that for a few seconds, glancing down when he heard the candle sputtering in its place on the floor and seeing a hairy spider scurry past it. "Then we'll have to start with those three," he finally said with a sigh. "Have they got names?"

"Probably."

"Good," said Slocum. "And do you, by chance, happen to know what they are?"

The blonde glanced toward the door, some of the fear returning to her eyes. She had forgotten to be frightened for a while, but now the significance of what she was doing came back to her. "Say, mister, who the hell are you anyway?"

"Just a friend of the Lazy K," he said, his lips twisting into a tight grin. "Someone who tried to get their cows back and had a fine pony shot out from under him."

She glanced at the doorway again and then studied his face.

"Just a minute," said Slocum. He put his hands on the butts of his Colt Navies, one in its holster and the spare stuffed in his pants, and stepped through the doorway, quickly searched the darkness with his eyes and his ears, then came back to the girl. "No one's listening, Julie. And I promise you we won't make it real obvious that we have all this information."

"Just save that stuff, mister. You don't give a shit about me."

"Well, maybe not much of one. But more than you think." Slocum sighed. "Look, we'll probably catch up with them just by trailing the herd. I'm only trying to get an idea of what we're up against."

The blonde frowned thoughtfully, then shrugged her shoulders. "I guess I'm in deep enough as it is," she said. "I just hope you remember to come get me out of this hellhole."

"I will."

"I bet. Anyway, I only know about the three of them that I mentioned, and they sure ain't worth much as outlaws. They'll probably shoot you dead if you put 'em in a corner, but they ain't all that mean. No one knows where they came from."

"Names?"

"Riley's one of them, probably the day-to-day boss. And then there's—"

"What's Riley look like?"

"Oh, kind of small, but real wiry, with blond hair about the color of mine and practically as long. Then there's a guy they call Coco, a Mex who's a little taller than Riley but kind of pudgy. He's got a knife scar right below his . . . let's see, his right eye. And then there's Smith—"

"He probably thought long and hard to come up with a name like that."

"It's the one he uses," Julie said with a shrug. "I don't see him much."

"Doesn't he like girls?"

"Not me, anyway. He keeps to himself, doesn't talk much. He's almost as tall as you are, but his hair is brown and his ears stick out kind of funny."

"A charming little family," Slocum said. "Do they live around here?"

The blonde looked at the doorway again. "Now wait a minute. If you went there, then they'd know it was me for sure."

"Calm down, Julie. We can also just watch the place and follow them from there, if we can't find their trail in the canyon. We'll make trouble for 'em somewhere else so they'll never be sure how we got on to them."

The girl opened her mouth and left it open for a moment, staring into the night, as if she needed time to gather her courage. "It's on the north side of town," she finally said in a small voice. "They put a stove in, so you'll see the pipe comin' up through the roof. They've also got some deer horns nailed on the door." She hugged herself and shivered, then looked up at Slocum. "Will you really come? And take me somewhere else?"

Slocum grinned and said, "At least you haven't lost all hope."

"Give me another year or two for that," she grunted.

"I suppose. How old are you, anyway?"

"Eighteen."

Slocum stared down at the blonde, feeling sad and feeling the years that had slipped by. He nodded his head after a while and sighed deeply. "Yeah," he said, "we'll be back for you. Now wipe that frightened look off your face and let's go back inside."

"You better put a satisfied look on *your* face," said the blonde. "Like the only thing you got from me was a good time."

"Speaking of which," said Slocum. He pulled two gold coins out of his pocket and gave her the bigger of the two, then changed his mind and gave her the second one as well.

"Fifteen dollars!" said the girl, her eyes going wide. "Why would you—"

"Call it insurance," Slocum said. "If I get shot or break a leg . . . well, maybe you'll be able to bribe someone else to take you where you want to go."

"Thanks, mister."

"Thank *you*. Now, stop looking like you're about to cry and let's get back to the saloon."

10

"You took your goddamn time," Boyd murmured when Slocum returned to the table. "I suppose you've noticed the new arrivals."

"I see them," Slocum said. The gravity of his tone didn't match the dreamy smile he was faking as he watched the blonde sidle up to a slim rawboned man sitting at a table across the room. Slocum's smile changed slightly, reflecting a glint of humor in his eyes. "And my time was well spent, Mitch. No need to get jealous just because she picked me instead of you."

"I suppose you're flattered, Slocum. After all, it's been my life's ambition to go out back with some cheap little whore."

Boyd's expression was sour but Slocum saw the trace of a grin at the corners of his mouth, and knew it was safe to continue. "I can get her back over here if you want—as a favor to a friend. Do you need to borrow any money?"

Boyd laughed. "Maybe tomorrow, Slocum. Right now I think we should concentrate on the two gents who are lookin' us over. They came back with the fella that scooted out of here when we first come in."

"You mean the two that are getting up and heading this way?" said Slocum. "The ones who look like they've been breaking rocks at Leavenworth for the last ten years?"

"That's a pretty accurate description," Boyd whispered casually, trying hard not to show that he was nervous. "Do we leave now or just shoot them or what?"

"I'm not sure a ball could get through all that muscle," Slocum said. "I'm afraid it might bounce off."

"You mean about like our fists would?"

"It may not be any fun," Slocum said wistfully, shaking his head, "but you got to admit there're some benefits to spending time in a penitentiary."

"If it comes to a choice, I think I'd still rather shoot one of them than try to hit him with my hands."

"Let's hope we get a choice."

Slocum and Boyd finally looked up when the hardcases stopped a few feet away from their table. The one in front had yellowish eyes and rotting teeth. "Where did you two come from?" said the man.

"What makes that any of your business?" Slocum said.

"Because you killed a friend of mine, for one thing."

Slocum realized that Frank's body had been removed while he was in the back room with Julie. Now there was only a splash of blood seeping slowly into the hard-packed dirt floor. Some of it would dry up first, leaving a patch that would look like a large scab on the earth.

"Your friend was drawin' down on me at the time," Slocum said calmly. "He didn't leave me much choice."

"That's what I hear," said the man, curling his lip. "It's about the only reason you ain't dead already."

"You wouldn't find it all that easy," Slocum said coldly.

"Yeah, I heard you're fast," the man admitted. "I also heard there was a pack of shit-kickers on their way up the canyon today."

"Are you part of the shit we were coming to kick?"

Slocum saw the man clench his massive, bony fist at his side, his yellow eyes flaring. "Goddamn if you don't take serious chances," he breathed.

Slocum didn't answer, thinking about what he'd just learned. There had to be a reason the man refused to rise to Slocum's bait, which was probably that he had something else in mind. Slocum kept staring at the man but also let his vision blur just a little to cover the rest of the room. The other customers had stopped what they were doing to watch the entertainment, and were sitting very still now, afraid they would miss something if they moved. The silence stretched a moment or two longer. Slocum was aware that he could hear nothing but the low hiss of the lanterns burning in the room. He almost jumped when the man with the yellow eyes finally spoke.

"The reason I ask," he began, biting off the words with forced civility, "I don't notice any horses outside. I see you here, but I don't see how you got here."

"Like I said, what the hell business is it of yours?"

"Because we don't like strangers!" bellowed the man, leaning forward suddenly and giving Slocum a full view of his rotten teeth. "Especially smart-ass ones who could mean trouble for the people here."

Slocum stared up at the man, unflinching, and when he spoke again his voice was so quietly level that it was almost a whisper. "Did you shoot my horse?" he asked.

The man snapped up straight, his face ugly with hatred and his big fist clenching automatically at his side.

"If you didn't," Slocum said calmly, "then you got nothing to worry about."

"I ain't worried," the big man spat out harshly. "It's you that oughta be worried." He glanced around the saloon, once again getting a grip on himself. "But the boys here are gonna give you a chance to leave quietly —and alive."

"On foot?" said Slocum. "In the middle of the night?"

"The moon'll be up pretty quick, and we got horses

for you." The man offered a wicked, taunting grin, as if to challenge Slocum. "We got plenty of horses, from all over this territory."

Slocum glanced at Boyd, hoping that the red-haired man also smelled the makings of a trap, because he wanted to walk into it to see what would happen. He also wanted horses.

"What kind of price are you putting on these ponies?" he asked, as if he thought he was being shrewd.

"The price is that you get out of our hair."

"Fair enough," Slocum said, giving Boyd another look. "Mitch, how about you dig out our gear and get it ready. I'll bring the horses around as soon as I see what we're being offered."

Boyd nodded shortly, meeting Slocum's eye but not giving any hint of whether he understood Slocum's purpose: that Boyd stay free so he could continue keeping an eye on Slocum's back. They stood in unison, their chair legs scraping grooves in the dirt and the big outlaws stepping back to make room. Boyd stepped into the night without another word and Slocum still wasn't sure whether he was going to get the saddles or double back and watch.

The outlaws had taken a coal-oil lamp off one end of the bar and stopped to wait by the back door. Slocum joined them there, meeting their cold stares and deciding to act as if he was on his own. They didn't seem concerned that Boyd was going off somewhere else, but he also noticed that the man who carried the lantern— the one who hadn't spoken yet, whose gun was on his right hip—was using his left hand. Slocum's own fingers were never far from the butt of his Colt as the three men crunched over the hard ground, hemmed in by the blackness that surrounded their little floating pool of light. Slocum keyed up his nerves to the slightest suspicious movement or rustle of sound from either of his companions. He kept a foot or two apart from them, leaving himself room to move if they should seem to threaten him. He also stayed close enough, he hoped, to eliminate the threat of shots ripping out of the night. Even so, he kept half an eye on the looming shapes of the buildings they passed, and watched the deep shadows beside them for any warning glints or flashes.

Time seemed to go into a slow crawl for Slocum, jammed with dozens of sounds and smells and the chill desert air touching his flesh. It felt like the whole night had gone by, instead of a few seconds, when the three men came up to the wooden building with the barn door that Slocum had pointed out earlier. Now Slocum could hear the sound of horses munching hay behind the door, and smell the sharp smell of their piss. The man with the lantern held it higher while the one with the rotten teeth lifted a latch on the door.

"We got some nags in here that ought to suit you," he said unpleasantly. "With any luck they'll get you all the way to Chandlerville before they crap out."

"That's generous," Slocum said dryly.

"Hey! When you consider the alternative," the man snapped, swinging the big door open wide. "Just shut up and be happy with what you get."

The two outlaws went on into the barn, casually, without looking back, and Slocum followed them with a puzzled frown. He walked slowly, looking into each stall and behind each beam, quickly falling behind the outlaws.

"Come on!" the big one said impatiently. "Ain't nothing here but horses."

"I didn't get to this advanced age by believing everything I hear," Slocum said, taking his time. When he caught up, about halfway down the livery barn, the bandits were standing in front of three well-used horses. Even in the dim, uneven lanternlight Slocum could see their matted hair, as if they'd been lathered up and still hadn't had a chance to roll it out in the dust. The ponies stood with their heads hanging listlessly, barely turning for a glance at the men.

Slocum wasn't looking at them very closely—most of his attention was still focused on listening and trying to *feel* everything around him in the barn—but something about the horses began to tug at his attention. He focused on the Appaloosa first, then studied the other two. A bay and a roan. His mind flashed back to the time he and Rachel had gone pounding over the rise, seeing the brilliance of the desert sunset and underneath it the rustlers herding the cattle up toward the canyon.

They had been riding an Appaloosa and a bay and roan.

Slocum glanced at the outlaws beside him, directly into the yellow eyes that were studying him with a blank look which might have been contempt or hatred. They were staring at each other when Slocum heard a struggle outside.

"I wouldn't if I were you," said the outlaw, reading Slocum's eyes in the instant before he reached for his gun.

Slocum's Colt was already halfway out of its holster before he thought better of it, warned by something in the outlaw's calm, confident manner.

"We got him!" came a voice from outside. "We're comin' in."

"See what I mean?" said the outlaw, his rotten teeth showing in an insolent grin. "One false step from you and your friend's a dead man. Now let that pistol drop back where it came from."

Slocum hesitated, his eyes and the outlaw's eyes still locked together as if they were the only two men in the world. He heard other men coming up behind him and knew the situation was hopeless, but at the same time he remembered fighting his way out of equally hopeless situations when he was riding with Quantrill. He was

still staring into the bandit's yellow eyes, feeling
trapped and helpless and hating the feeling, and slowly
the hatred for the feeling became a hatred for the grinning yellow-eyed son of a bitch who was standing in
front of him, refusing to look away, knowing he had the
upper hand. The hatred became a fury building inside
him, so strong that he almost pulled the Colt anyway,
hearing someone being dragged into the barn behind
him.

Then a calmer voice seemed to call from a great distance inside his head, telling him that the outlaws had
already had their chance to kill him. *Play the odds for
now,* said the voice. The balance tipped and Slocum
carefully unwrapped his fingers from around the butt of
his revolver. His hands and arms seemed to float out
away from his sides, as if they didn't belong to him.

The outlaw in front of him reached for the gun, his
grin even wider now. "Pretty smart," he said, "for
someone so stupid."

Slocum's arms still seemed to have a life of their
own. One moment he was looking into the outlaw's
taunting face and the next instant he saw his own fist
crashing into the man's nose, blood splattering every-
where as the man's head snapped back under the force
of the blow. Then he caught a movement in the corner
of his eye, and before he could turn he felt the crash of a
gun butt against the base of his skull.

Slocum smelled dirt. He wondered vaguely why the
odor was so strong, as if the dirt was just underneath his
nose. He wondered about it for what seemed like a long
time, turning it over in his mind, before he realized that
his cheek was pressed against something hard and gritty.
A little while later it came to him that the two facts
might be related. Maybe he was lying face down in the
dirt somewhere. But why?

He struggled with that, slipping in and out of the

effort, until suddenly he was seeing pictures against his closed eyelids. The saloon. The blonde. The walk toward the livery. The blood squirting from Yellow-Eyes' nose.

Slocum's own eyes snapped open, his eyelashes brushing the dirt, but there was no change in his vision. He was either blind or in total darkness. With a sudden sense of urgency he tried to jerk himself to his hands and knees, only to cry out loud with pain and settle back to the ground.

"Take it easy, partner," said a groggy voice behind him.

Slocum rested a moment, a feeling of relief washing over him when he realized the voice belonged to Mitch Boyd. But he was also getting furious as he started remembering exactly where the pain had come from, and why.

"He kicked you a couple times," Boyd said softly, as if he could read Slocum's mind. "The other one whacked you on the head and then the one whose nose you busted . . . he gave you a couple good shots in the ribs."

Slocum thought about it, breathing hard and smelling the dust but feeling a little afraid even to twitch a muscle. It seemed right, what Boyd said. He could separate it out now. There had been a sharp crease of pain across the top of his head, and an even sharper one that burned along his side. He had nearly blacked out again. *I'm getting tired of this shit,* he thought.

"Your ribs feel okay," Boyd murmured. "I mean, I don't think any of 'em's broken. They prob'ly don't feel so great to you."

Slocum discovered he could move his lips without hurting anything. "What about you?" he asked. "Any damage?"

"Mostly just tired," Boyd said with a dispirited sigh. *"My* ribs got jabbed with a scattergun, but not so hard.

Just enough to keep me humble when they were bringin'
me to the barn."

"They jumped you?"

"Yeah," Boyd sighed. "I'm sorry, Slocum. I was circling back, tryin' to get a fix on you, and they were
waiting. I ran right into 'em."

"It's not your fault," Slocum said. "We were looking
for a trap but we didn't happen to look in the place they
were setting it. They plain outsmarted us. And your
eyes didn't even get a chance to adjust to the dark."

"Well, shit, I still should have—"

"Are we in the barn now?" Slocum interrupted.

"Nope. One of those adobes on the plaza."

"How long?"

"Christ, I don't know. I felt around for a while, trying to find a hole or a window or a crack. Some way to
get us out of here. But it's solid fuckin' mud, Slocum,
and they put a sheet of tin over the door. Which has its
hinges on the outside, by the way." Boyd sighed again
and then said, "Christ, I just gave up and went to sleep
. . . until you woke me up with that holler."

Slocum stirred very slowly, pivoting on his shoulder
and shifting his weight until he was lying on his back,
looking straight up. He wasn't sure whether he saw or
only felt the other man's shape hunched up against a
wall.

"It's still dark as far as I can tell," Boyd added. "I
figure sleepin' is about the only thing that makes any
sense after the short night and long day we had. Not to
mention your gettin' knocked on the head twice."

Slocum closed his eyes and his head swam a little as
he listened to the memory of Boyd's voice. "You sound
like you really have given up," Slocum said.

"I admit I ain't exactly filled with hope. Should I
be?"

"Well, for one thing, the man stopped kicking me.
And the shotgun in your ribs didn't go off."

"Yet."

"What better chance could they have?" Slocum argued.

"Maybe they're waiting for orders. Maybe they want information."

It was Slocum's turn to sigh, although he forgot that taking a full breath would cause a stab of pain in his side. "You're not exactly a bundle of cheer," he said. "I'm gonna take your advice and go back to sleep before you convince me I should cut my own throat."

"Christ," said Boyd, sounding disgusted with himself. "I'm sorry, Slocum."

"Stop kicking yourself so hard and go to sleep!" Slocum said. "The mood you're in, you can't help feeling anything but better in the morning, no matter how hard you try."

Slocum thought he heard a short, dry laugh. He was going to say something else, but his head was swimming again and his eyes felt heavy and then he was dreaming about the noise and blood and heat of war—the evil guerrilla war he fought with Quantrill—where you kept advancing and never even thought about giving up.

Or maybe the dream came in the morning, when he woke up to a steady scraping sound. He opened his eyes on a small stream of light coming through a crack beneath the door, as well as a few other cracks or pinholes, and when he pivoted his head to the side he could see Mitch Boyd crouched on his knees against a wall. His shoulders were moving with a rhythm that matched the scraping sound.

Slocum eased himself up onto an elbow, discovering that there was little more than a pounding ache in his side and his head. "I thought you'd given up," he said cheerfully.

Boyd jumped and then turned around and sat down

on the ground, grinning at Slocum as he wiped his forehead with a dirt-caked hand. Slocum saw that his
fingernails were torn and bloody. "You musta been
dreamin'," said the redhead. "We Boyds never know
when to give up."

"Be nice if everything else was just a dream."

"Yeah." Boyd was looking somber again. "It's been
light two or three hours now, Slocum, and no one's
come by to feed us or even see if we're still alive. Like
they don't much care whether we are or not."

"I'm sure they don't," Slocum said. "But we are."

"But they can't afford to let us leave, can they?"

Slocum shrugged. "All they were shooting at yesterday was horses."

Boyd nodded thoughtfully, then frowned. "None of it
makes sense, I'll give you that. But this business of not
bothering to feed us—that bothers me. I don't feel like
waiting around to see what happens."

"I'm with you," said Slocum, getting to his feet as
Boyd turned back to the wall. The redhead was gouging
one of the adobe bricks with his fingers, scraping and
digging in with his fingernails and prying out small peb-
bles and pieces of straw—whatever seemed to work.
There was a hole in the dark brown mud about the size
of Boyd's fist.

"What would you say?" Slocum asked. "Three or
four inches deep?"

Boyd nodded, scraping and prying.

"And the average adobe wall is what, a foot and a
half?"

"I'm tryin' not to think about it, Slocum. That's why
I'm workin' on this wall, so I don't have to sit around
and think."

Slocum studied Boyd's work, deciding the fist-sized
hole represented no more time than the two or three
hours of daylight he'd mentioned. Probably less, since it
was the lack of breakfast that apparently worried him
enough to get started. In his mind, Slocum doubled the

size of the hole, representing the effort of two men, and then multiplied that by four or five, representing the amount of daylight they probably had left.

It didn't amount to much of a hole.

Slocum stretched and began to stroll along the wall, studying it carefully, examining the door when he came to it, and looking up at the big wooden beams that supported the thatched roof. The beams were set solidly in the adobe, and even though the roof itself didn't look as formidable as the wall, it was too far out of reach. Neither one of them would be able to hold the other up there long enough to do anything useful.

Slocum went back to stand over Boyd, feeling through his own pockets and around his waist. The bandits had taken everything he owned, even his belt. He cursed aloud when he realized that his hat was gone, with its band of silver conchos. But the immediate problem was that neither one of them had anything they could use for tools. Boyd had already accepted the fact and started digging anyway. Slocum admired the man's spirit, picturing once again the hole he thought they might be able to dig by nightfall. Finally he doubled *that,* figuring they could dig through the night if they had to.

"Well, hell," Slocum finally said with a sigh, settling to his knees beside Boyd. "I guess it ain't totally hopeless. Maybe they won't get the orders to shoot us till tomorrow."

"Sure," said Boyd, picking at the wall and grunting with the pain and effort. "And all they'll find is a hole. We'll outsmart them by dying of thirst in the desert."

Slocum laughed. "No wonder you gave up prospecting, Mitch. You're a pessimist by nature, and you gotta have *hope* if you're planning to go around hunting for gold."

"That's me, Slocum. No hope . . . but I don't know when to give up."

"Like staying at the Lazy K for two years."

Boyd faltered for a second and Slocum knew he had touched a sore spot. "Those bastards," said the redhead.

"The whole family?" Slocum asked, surprised. "Or are we talking about the men who put us in here?"

"Almost comes to the same thing, don't it? But no, I guess I'm just talkin' about the so-called men in that family. We wouldn't be in this fix if those two were— hell, I bet Rachel *could* handle the place better than they can."

"I thought a woman's job was just to cook and sew."

Boyd glanced up from his digging and grinned when he saw Slocum's smile. "Well, then," he said, "most women. I gotta admit Rachel's had some pretty good ideas about the way things oughta be done. She's been sayin' we should hire stock detectives right from the beginning, when we first started missin' cows."

"Kevin and the old man didn't like the idea?"

"I think Kevin's afraid of Stonetown. He kept sayin' the thefts would probably stop anyway, and we didn't want to stir up a lot of trouble that would make enemies for the ranch."

"That's interesting," Slocum said, frowning thoughtfully. "Julie told me the rustlers were planning to quit pretty soon, so Kevin was right about that part of it... except I can't see why he'd be so sure."

"I always figured he was just a coward," Boyd said with a shrug. "Just a bunch of wishful thinkin' on his part."

"Why do you think the old man went along? He seems flinty enough."

"You bet he is. He built that spread out of nothing. But the talk is that he doesn't want to make the sheriff look bad."

"Henry Wingfield?" said Slocum. "Rachel mentioned something about that."

"Well, those two practically settled this country by themselves. Now Wingfield is gettin' old, and there's some in the county who say he's *too* old. The election is coming up sometime an' I guess Mr. Anderson feels like it would be a slap in the face if he hired outside help. So he keeps hopin' his old friend and the deputies will make some arrests."

"No such luck?"

Boyd shook his head, still scraping with his bloody fingernails. "Kevin keeps hoping—whatever his reasons are—and he doesn't do a damn thing. His father goes along with it, out of friendship for an old has-been. So here *we* are, tryin' to fight their battles for 'em, and we end up scrapin' our goddamned fingers raw on the goddamn *off*-chance that it'll keep us from gettin' killed, and they're probably sittin' down to a hot lunch right about now. Steak and biscuits and gravy."

"You don't sound like you're having fun any more."

"You're goddamn right I'm—"

Boyd stopped suddenly and stared up at Slocum for several seconds, then laughed out loud. "I guess you should have kicked me last night, when I started talking about havin' fun. I always remember havin' great fun later on, once I'm out of a scrape. But it never seems so great at the time, does it? Mostly you're just sore or scared."

"Or both," said Slocum, looking down at his own raw fingers. "Usually both."

"I swear, Slocum, if I ever get out of this I'm gonna find a nice job clerkin' in a dry-goods store somewhere."

"Are you forgetting about Rachel?"

"Not even for a second. I wish to hell she'd come with me." Boyd let out a long sigh. "It's the only thing I've wanted for two years . . . maybe even the only thing I ever *really* wanted. I don't mean the dry-goods store, of course. I mean Rachel, and a place of our own, and prob'ly a couple kids. Don't that sound good to you?"

Slocum nodded wordlessly, unaware that he had

stopped scraping and was staring into the wall as if he could see through it. "There was a time when I felt exactly the same way," he said after a while. "I even had the place, a good farm back in Georgia. Been in the family three generations."

"What happened?"

"Someone took it away," Slocum said, snapping out the words with a bitterness that surprised him. "I mean he tried. I killed the bastard, but in a way he won."

"Damn! I'm sorry to hear it, Slocum."

Slocum shrugged and went back to work. "Who knows?" he said. "Maybe I was kidding myself. Maybe I would have left anyway. I sure haven't stayed put anywhere since."

There was an awkward silence for a few minutes as the men worked side by side, making the hole wider and deeper and listening for any sounds on the other side or beyond the wooden door. Then their silence was comfortable, a product of concentrating on the task and also trying to ignore the pain and apprehension.

No one ever came to the adobe, and it was Slocum who suggested that they might raise suspicions by their silence. They took turns beating on the door for a few minutes, yelling out for food and help, then yelling "Fire!" All the demands and tricks that might be expected of prisoners. Then they went back to the wall.

Sometimes they cursed in frustration. Other times they made jokes at the expense of outlaws or ranchers or sheriff's deputies. Much later they began to notice a gradual dimming of the light, and before long they were unable to see each other's faces even though each of them could feel the warm tickle of the other man breathing on his neck or cheek.

"Maybe we oughta get married to *each other* after this is over," Boyd said during the night.

"No offense, Mitch, but I think I'll have had enough of you."

They spoke less and less through the night, and when they did speak their words were slurred by exhaustion and lack of food. Mostly they focused on the repeated act of sheer will which allowed them to put their tortured fingers back in the hole and keep digging, ignoring the dull agony minute by minute. They allowed themselves short naps of a few minutes each, taking turns so they could wake each other up. Sometimes Slocum felt so painfully alone, when Boyd was asleep, that tears stung his eyes. But it seemed as if his entire life had narrowed down to the hole in the adobe, and so he felt a lyrical happiness whenever he reached his hand inside, almost up to his elbow, and felt around in a space that would allow his shoulders to pass—if he twisted one arm up over his head.

In the end he almost let out a whoop of joy when he kicked through the last few inches of dirt, feeling a fresh breeze on his bare foot, and looked out on the little settlement in the first grey light of dawn.

11

Slocum went first, squeezing through with one arm pressed up tight against his ear. He had to curl his lips to blow falling dirt off his face and out of his eyes. He stopped with his head just outside the wall and twisted his neck to look around, examining the two other adobes he could see, then bent his knees in a predetermined signal to tell Boyd the area was clear.

It was a strange moment that he would never forget, staring along the rough adobe wall that seemed to begin at his chin while another part of his body was moving inside the house. He knew that without sleep the mind begins playing tricks, but the knowledge didn't make it any less startling to suddenly believe, just for a second, that his body had actually split into two separate parts: his head and arm dangling from the wall out in the coming daylight, and the rest of him inside the dark prison.

The spell was broken when he felt Boyd grab hold of his legs and start to push, while Slocum wiggled his shoulders and chest through the hole. Soon his other arm was free, and then his hips, and then it was easy. He padded unsteadily to the corner of the house, where he once again went down on his knees.

The house fronted on the little open space across from the saloon, where a man with a shotgun was leaning back in a chair beside the door. The door itself was closed and there was no sign of light behind it, but the

man with the shotgun was wide awake, little more than
a shadow in the deep dusk. He seemed to be looking off
to the right when Slocum eased his head around the
corner at ground level, and quickly pulled it back. He
sat for a moment, studying the distribution of the buildings he could see, as well as the hill that rose gently
behind them. Then he crept to the other corner of the
wall.

All he could see there was a few more scattered
buildings, with closed doors and wooden shutters to
cover the rare windows. No guards. No sleeping
drunks. Slocum nodded with satisfaction and went back
to the hole, kneeling down to see Boyd's haggard face
in the opening.

"You look just beautiful in the morning," Slocum
whispered. "Come on out and join me."

Boyd followed Slocum's example, coming out head-
and-arm-first, with Slocum tugging at his arm to help
him along. The redhead was chunkier than Slocum and
he had a few seconds of panic when his chest seemed to
lodge firmly in the hole. Slocum calmed him down and
told him to get rid of all the air in his lungs, and after a
few seconds Boyd was able to try it. A few seconds
after that he was on his feet.

Slocum pointed the way and the two men walked
silently on bare feet toward the back of the building,
where they crossed to the back of another and still another, working their way around to the saloon. They had
been hearing noise through most of the night, shouting
and drunken laughter and two or three shots, but apparently everyone except the guard was now asleep.

Julie's door behind the saloon was cracked open.
Slocum's heart sank and for a moment he was afraid to
open it any more. The people of Stonetown seemed to
be a rougher bunch than he had given them credit for
when he first spoke to her. He motioned Boyd to stand
on the other side of the door, both men flat against the

wall, while he nudged it with his fingertips. He peered in cautiously when no shots came, barely able to distinguish the girl's body on the pile of bedding—and a much larger body beside hers.

After a quick look around, Slocum eased toward the bed with Boyd not far behind, scanning the floor and walls for something to use as a weapon. The girl didn't seem to own anything bigger than a hand mirror, but the breathing of the man beside her was heavy and slow, more like the groggy unconsciousness of liquor than real sleep. He was also fully clothed, as if he had come here to guard against the girl's escape. Slocum didn't recognize him. He clenched his fist, frowning at the torn and blood-caked skin on his fingers before flexing them several times above the holstered gun on the sleeping man's hip. Then he glanced up at Boyd, who nodded. Slocum scooped the pistol out of its holster and raised it above the man's head, all in one smooth motion, smashing the pistol butt down just above the outlaw's shirt collar.

The outlaw's body jerked once, then lay still again. Boyd had lunged to put his hand over the girl's mouth and now she was struggling frantically beneath it, her eyes wide with terror until she recognized Slocum, who put his finger to his lips. The girl stared at him, her eyes gleaming white above Boyd's huge dirt-crusted hand. Slocum saw that one of the eyes was discolored, with an ugly cut above it on her forehead. When Boyd removed his hand they could both see the wide split on her lip, and her swollen jaw.

Slocum scowled and raised the gun above the outlaw's head again, but the blonde put up her hand. "It wasn't him," she whispered. "He was just keeping an eye on me, and he passed out."

Slocum grumbled softly, wanting to at least hit something, until it came to him that he was partly mad at himself for putting the girl in danger. He rolled the outlaw on his back and began unbuckling his gunbelt, first pointing at the man's boots for Boyd's benefit. "They ought to fit you," he whispered. "But don't put 'em on just yet. Julie, you get some riding clothes on."

Slocum sent Boyd around to the far side of the saloon, waiting at the near side until he heard a muttered curse. In his mind he saw Boyd popping around the corner as they'd planned, then cursing and retreating as if he'd made a mistake. In the next instant Slocum had slipped around his own corner, running silently in bare feet. The outlaw had his back turned, twisting toward Boyd and coming out of his chair, its front legs thudding in the dirt. By the time he heard Slocum running up behind him he just had time to swing the barrel of his shotgun before he felt the crunch of his skull under metal. He was thinking that he should have yelled something, more or less at the same time that his legs were folding beneath him and the shotgun left his hands.

Slocum had grabbed its barrel as it was coming around, and held onto it as the man crumpled. "Thanks," he murmured to the fallen bandit, recognizing him now as Yellow-Eyes' partner. "Glad to repay the favor."

Boyd poked his head back around the corner, and when he came up Slocum handed him the shotgun so he could cover the plaza. Then Slocum knelt quickly and unbuckled his own gunbelt at the outlaw's waist. It felt good to have at least one of his Navies back on his hip. He checked the loads and then pulled off the outlaw's boots, carrying them back around the corner to the girl's room, where he and Boyd both put on their borrowed footwear.

"Goddamn!" Boyd said, his voice a harsh whisper but his face split by a wide grin. "I sure am feelin' lucky all of a sudden. This is where it starts gettin' fun again, Slocum."

"Then it's my turn to be the pessimist," Slocum said.

"Don't forget that we only got ten shots between us—"

"Plus the two in the scattergun."

"Yeah, but we still better make 'em count. If it comes to that."

"I hope it does," Boyd whispered, his mouth curling into an ugly expression.

"Even if it's two against God knows how many?"

Boyd scowled, shaking his head, then offered a rueful grin. "Maybe I'm feelin' too lucky for my own good."

"I wouldn't mind sticking around long enough to get my conchos back," Slocum admitted, "and a few other things. But mostly I want a good horse between my legs and a couple dozen miles between me and Stonetown. I think that's the wisest idea."

"Amen!" said Boyd.

The blonde only nodded when Slocum looked at her.

"Anyone likely to be in the saloon?" he asked her.

This time she shook her head.

"What about weapons?"

"I think that was it," she said, nodding toward the shotgun. "I think they kept it behind the bar."

"I sure wish we had a little more firepower," Slocum said thoughtfully.

"Maybe the girl knows where some of these characters sleep," Boyd suggested. "By themselves."

Slocum shook his head without even looking at her. "I'd hate to risk even one shot, Mitch. Then we'd have the whole damn town on our tails, coming at us from God knows where, and we'd still be a long way from help. Come on."

Slocum scouted ahead and then all three scuttled quietly across the plaza toward the corral behind the livery barn. Boyd brought up the rear with the shotgun and covered the plaza while Slocum and Julie opened the gate. The darkness was fading quickly into dawn and Slocum was feeling more urgency now than ever, but he had to move carefully past the ten or twelve horses standing inside the corral.

"Can you ride without a saddle?" he asked the girl.

"I can hang on."

"That's about all any of us can do," Slocum said with a grim smile. "I'll try to find some bridles, or at least a hackamore."

He drew his Colt and opened the back door all the way, to admit as much light as possible. Nothing jumped out. He found what he wanted hanging from nails on the main support beams, as well as four more horses in stalls. He looked them over for a moment and decided that three of them were as good as anything he might find in the corral. Working as fast but as quietly as he could, he began slipping bits into their mouths.

When he was done Slocum freed the fourth pony and drove it out the back door, leading the other three behind him and motioning to the girl to open the gate again. Boyd appeared at the corner, having followed Slocum's progress with his ears, and now he climbed through the poles to take the reins for one of the horses, a big grey, and hop onto its back. Slocum put his arms around Julie's waist and hoisted her onto a little mustang, then hoisted himself onto a buckskin that seemed to have a little spirit.

The two men glanced at each other and wordlessly took up positions on either side of the girl, Slocum holding his Colt and Boyd the scattergun, with a pistol in reserve. They moved up behind the other horses in the corral and began waving their arms, herding them toward open range but still keeping an eye on the sleeping town. Slocum was thinking that the horses would probably return quickly enough anyway, wanting to stay near water, which meant that the three fugitives would have to ride full out if they hoped to get away. It promised to be another long, hot, pounding day, and thinking about it distracted Slocum for a few seconds.

He started paying attention again when he heard the bark of two rifles, one near and one far away.

"Shit," said Slocum, going limp with a sense of absolute hopelessness. But it only lasted a second or two. By then he had caught the movement behind a water trough across the plaza, where a man was rising up and collapsing at the same time, his rifle going off in the dirt, and also the movement on a hilltop seventy or eighty yards above Stonetown. Slocum nudged the girl and pointed toward the figures on the hill waving their arms, then slapped her horse on the rump and kicked his own.

"Good Lord," he said once they were running, "do you see what I see, Mitch?"

"I hope you mean the red hair," said Boyd. "I'd hate to think I was indulging in fantasies at a time like this."

"You never seen a rider with hair that long, have you?"

The people on the hill were still waving, and suddenly Slocum understood.

"They want us to get away from the horses," he said.

Boyd looked puzzled for a moment, and then he was grinning again. "Let's go!" he shouted.

Slocum didn't feel quite so excited as the three of them veered off, racing their mounts toward the hill beneath a shattering volley of rifle fire, the slugs whistling over their heads. Almost immediately he began to hear the squealing of the horses as they were shot down. He looked back once, but even in the name of revenge he could take no pleasure in the kicking and thrashing of dying animals.

Julie also risked a backward glance, hugging the mustang's neck for all she was worth. "My God!" she screamed. "Why are they doing that? We could have driven them up the hill."

One of the saloon customers appeared in a doorway at the edge of town. Slocum snapped off a couple of shots and the man disappeared back inside. "It's partly revenge for what happened in the canyon," he yelled across to the girl. "Giving them a taste of their own—"

"But they still wouldn't have had any horses! We could have taken our time driving them back, because there's no way they could have chased us."

Slocum nodded, the girl's questions forcing his weary mind to follow her logic. He felt even more weary when he came to the only conclusion possible.

"I doubt we're going back," he said. "I have a feeling we'll be trying to track the herd."

He saw an explosion of dirt ahead of him and yelled "Stay low!" to the girl, then smiled at the pointlessness of his advice. She was still clinging to her pony's neck and she wouldn't be able to get any lower unless she knew how to ride hanging from the side of her mount, Indian-style. The skill would have come in handy right then. More and more bullets were slicing through the air around them as the outlaws came out of their sleep and got into the fight. But the Lazy K riders on the hill had taken cover behind rocks and brush and were returning the fire hot and heavy, spoiling the bandits' aim.

That was what Slocum hoped, anyway.

He led the way off to one side as they neared the top of the hill, to avoid the crossfire, and got his horse stopped somewhere on the other side, after he lost sight of Stonetown. He jumped down and helped Julie unlock her numb fingers so she could separate her arms and release the mustang's neck.

"I'm glad it was a short ride," she said, trying to be cheerful. But her lips were quivering and her teeth were knocking together. Slocum wrapped his arms around her just as Rachel Anderson ducked back from the crest of the hill. She stopped dead when she saw him, giving him a peculiar look as Mitch Boyd came up from behind.

"Mr. Boyd," Rachel said coolly. "It's good to see *you* again."

"Uh-oh," Julie whispered into Slocum's ear. "Who's that, your wife?"

Slocum laughed without meaning to, a nervous reaction to his exhaustion and the strange little scene that seemed to be developing. "No," he said, "that's the daughter of the rancher who owned those disappearing cows."

"The daughter!" Julie hissed, staring at the red-haired woman coming toward them. "You been messing around with the boss's *daughter?*"

"No!" Slocum said again, aware of Boyd listening behind him. "Don't go jumping to any conclusions. It's a long story."

"All about bad luck," Boyd muttered over his shoulder.

Slocum opened his mouth to say something, but Rachel Anderson was almost on top of them now. She tossed her head and hair back toward the hilltop and said, "They'll keep the scum pinned down for a few minutes. What I need to know is, how much longer can the three of you last?"

"Whoa," said Slocum. "Back up a second. How the hell did you get here?"

The woman half turned away for a second, almost stamping her foot with impatience. "You still want to talk?" she said. "Can't you ever just *act?*"

"Even the troops need to hear what's happening once in a while," Slocum said with a grin.

Rachel Anderson held his gaze, arms folded beneath her breasts, the sound of sporadic shots echoing back across the hill. A moment later she seemed to relax, most of the impatience and anger disappearing from her expression.

"We've been here all night," she said, "catching up on sleep and trying to decide what to do and waiting for daybreak to do it. It was a hell of a surprise to see your toes come popping out of that adobe!"

"Where's your father and your brother?"

The woman looked away. "My father still couldn't make it."

"I'm sorry, Rachel."

Another impatient gesture, after which she was still staring into the distance and almost talking to herself. "I don't think Kevin's incompetence helped. If anything, some of the life went out of him when they all came moping back in yesterday morning. Kevin went off to his room to sleep while my father sat in his chair looking out a window, and I got so angry it almost drove me crazy. I wanted to kill my brother for letting you go off alone. I finally got so mad"—a quick, almost shy glance at Slocum—"well, I didn't even think about what I was doing. I went down to the bunkhouse and told the boys to get another hour's sleep and then we'd be riding back. I woke my brother up and he told me I was crazy. I wanted to tell him a lot of things but I was afraid to get started, so I just said he could come or he didn't have to. It was up to him."

"Good for you!" Slocum said happily, picturing the scene. "I knew you had it in you. I just wish I'd been there to see it. What did your father say?"

"He tried to stop me," Rachel said, lowering her eyes for a moment. "It was hard to go against him. But I think . . . I *hope* he was secretly pleased, too. He sure perked back up when he heard that you two decided to march right into Stonetown after Kevin gave up." The hint of a smile had touched her lips, reflected in her eyes as she looked from Slocum to Boyd. "I'm sure you know that's what he'd have done, once."

There was a lull in the gunfire and Slocum heard Boyd's boots scuffling in the dirt. "Well, hell," said the man, "that was all Slocum's idea. I just followed along."

"With no one twisting his arm," said Slocum. "And if he hadn't been there I'd still be sitting in that little adobe, waiting to see what the bandits wanted to do to me. Take a look at his fingers, Miss Anderson. You got a man here that doesn't know how to quit."

"Aw, hell," said Boyd.

"Glad to hear it!" said Rachel. "Because we're still only two days behind and I want to keep going after that herd." She gave the blonde a hard stare.

"Oh," said Slocum, "this is Julie. She gave me some information that might help us . . . and you can see what it cost her."

"Gave you information," Rachel repeated dryly, looking the girl up and down. Then she took a closer look at the girl's cut and swollen face. "Well, we did bring some fresh horses, but we only saddled two of them. I never knew you'd be bringing a guest, Slocum."

"I guess I can keep riding bareback," he told her.

"We'll work something out. We might even leave Guttierez behind with his friends, now that he's got us past the sentries."

"Guttierez!" said Slocum. "So he is the one after all."

"I didn't like it that he let you get jumped," Rachel explained, "and I liked his story even less. I had one of the boys stuff a Winchester down the front of his pants while I asked him some more questions."

Slocum grinned and shook his head, listening to Boyd choking behind him, and wondered if the man's infatuation for Rachel Anderson would hold up under the new light in which he was seeing her.

"He said there were three men running off our stock," Rachel continued.

"Riley, Coco, and Smith," Slocum finished, and when the woman gave him a puzzled look, he nodded toward Julie. "She gave me descriptions, too, and mentioned a fourth man who might be in charge of the whole thing."

"Those are the names Guttierez gave me," Rachel said with a thoughtful frown, "but he didn't mention any fourth man. Maybe we ought to hang onto him after all." A moment later she seemed to shrug off her questions in favor of action. "Have I explained everything to your satisfaction, then?" she asked with exaggerated patience. "Are we ready to go *now?*"

Slocum and Boyd exchanged looks. "I suppose," Slocum said slowly. "Of course, it might take a while to find the trail. Can we hold off the—"

"Trail's found," snapped Rachel. "We had a chance to scout around up here before dark last night and we came across their holding pen. It looks like they'd collected a couple hundred head, maybe more. Three men are pushing them southeast. Toward Mesilla."

"That goes along with what Julie told me," said Slocum, feeling his excitement rising. "And I doubt they could get to Mesilla before tonight."

"Just about the time we will," said Rachel.

"Well, what are we waiting for?" Slocum said, enjoying Rachel's sudden laugh. "We better head 'em off before they even get there, or you'll never get your cattle sorted out."

The second half of the remark made Rachel look thoughtful again. "I'm not so sure about that, Slocum. It's the strangest thing. We looked all around the holding pen, really searched it good, and we never found a trace of any branding fires."

"But how else would the rustlers use their running irons?"

The woman shrugged.

"I can't imagine them showing up in town with a whole herd of Lazy K stock," said Slocum.

"Neither can I," said Rachel. "But what other explanation is there?"

12

The Mexican named Chavez grinned happily beneath his bandit mustache when he saw Slocum and Boyd duck over the crest of the hill. But the skinny one named Guttierez, sitting next to him with his hands tied behind his back and a bandana covering his mouth, looked more like a man who didn't expect to see another sunrise. He was led behind the hill and his ankles were tied with a length of rawhide that ran beneath his horse.

"Some have tried to rush the hill," Chavez was reporting to Rachel. "But they found no cover and now they have retreated to the building there by the barn."

Slocum looked where Chavez was pointing and said, "That's their saloon. They're probably holding a strategy meeting."

"I hope they just decide to get out of Stonetown," Rachel said. "That was another mistake of my . . . well, I guess my father let Kevin make it. We never should have tolerated this place. Even if they did leave us alone."

"I'd say the truce is over now," said Slocum. "If they don't decide to leave, you'll probably have a fight on your hands."

"If a fight is what they want," Rachel said grimly, "you can bet a fight is just what they'll get."

"I might even stick around to see it through," said

Slocum. "If you'd want my help, that is."

The woman looked at him closely for a moment, then raised her eyes to the top of his head as a mischievous gleam appeared in her eyes. "You finally lost your hat," she said. "I suppose you're hoping to get it back if you join in."

"That's enough of an incentive right there," he admitted.

"In the meantime, how would you and Mr. Boyd feel about a chance to shoot the place up a little while we get underway?"

The two men answered with smiles, and Rachel left them with a pair of Winchesters while she led the rest of the hands—with Julie getting a lot of attention in the middle of the bunch—down the other side of the hill and into an arroyo. The two men each emptied a tube of shells over the next few minutes, mostly for the vengeful satisfaction they got from seeing glass break and water troughs spring leaks. Their occasional shots would also leave the impression that the hill was still infested with attackers. But after they reloaded, Slocum suggested a cease-fire.

A deep silence settled over the little village, and finally two or three outlaws stepped tentatively through the door of the saloon. One of them was a large man with heavy muscles who was wearing Slocum's hat. The silver conchos reflected dimly in the first rays of the rising sun, as if to tantalize him. Then he thought about the big man kicking him two nights before, and when he threw the Winchester to his shoulder he wasn't very careful about where the shots went.

In fact, Slocum grinned when Yellow-Eyes grabbed his leg and fell back through the door.

Mitch Boyd saw the grin and felt himself shudder. "I'd sure hate to have you mad at *me*," he said.

They continued to wait, but the outlaws didn't show themselves for another half-hour. Slocum guessed that the fight had gone out of them as soon as they realized the horses were dead, and especially after they'd tried to rush the hill with no concealment to take advantage of. Slocum and Boyd could have kept them pinned down all day, probably. They had a clear field of fire on either end of town. Even if the bandits had organized and taken cover behind the outer buildings with the idea of flanking the two men on the hilltop, they would have taken heavy losses in the fifty or sixty yards of open running before they reached the safety of a wash or ravine. After they drove the curious outlaws back into the saloon a second time, Slocum and Boyd figured they had bought at least another half-hour's time and decided to ride off after the rest of the Lazy K band. They followed a wide and easy path churned up by an even larger herd of cattle than Slocum had expected, but he noticed that the loosened dirt showed the marks of only four or five following horses.

"Looks like she's thrown out some flankers," Slocum said, and was proven correct when they caught up about forty minutes and six miles later. They came over a ridge and stopped when they saw Rachel scouting far ahead with one of the Anglo hands. They recognized Tibo Chavez's stout form about half a mile out on the right, with one of the other Mexicans half a mile to the left. Three vaqueros remained in the middle with Guttierez and the blonde.

"You'd almost think she's been in the army," Boyd said, shaking his head in admiration.

"Still think she should stick to cooking?" Slocum asked.

Boyd shook his head again, with a puzzled frown. "I never would have believed this, Slocum. I still don't understand such . . . such *ability* in a woman."

"Look how much older she is than Kevin," Slocum said. "That's about how many years the boss thought he wouldn't get another kid to take over for him. He was

talking about it the other night . . . except I don't think
he really understands what happened."

"And you do?"

Slocum shrugged. "Just guessing. But it sure sounds
like he got her interested in something besides keeping
house and then changed his mind, only she didn't
change hers."

Boyd didn't respond immediately and when Slocum
looked over at him he saw a dreamy, far-away look in
the redhead's eyes.

"Could you imagine bein' married to a woman like
that?" Boyd said when he was aware of Slocum's look.
"Just think of all the things you could do."

"I doubt you'd be making all the decisions yourself,"
Slocum warned.

"Yeah, but think of the things you could accomplish,
workin' with her. The things you could *build* together."
Boyd's face suddenly went stiff, and he seemed to shake
himself. "But I forgot," he said coldly. "You've probably figured all that out already—way ahead of me."

"I don't want to build a goddamn thing," Slocum
snarled. "With anyone." He spurred his horse violently,
as if he could ride away from a quick rush of memories.
Boyd's talk had taken him back suddenly to the dreams
he himself had nurtured when he went back to Slocum's
Stand after the War, the same dreams of wanting to
build a fine home with a good, strong woman. She
might have been like his mother—or like Rachel Anderson. Then a Reconstruction judge had taken
everything away. "Maybe I wanted those things once,"
he said when Boyd caught up with him. "But no more."

Only then did he notice the redhead's startled look of
surprise, which made him aware of just how much pain
his memories were causing him—and also that he was
taking it out on Boyd for accidently causing the memories to return.

"I'm sorry," Slocum said with a weak smile. "Just a

few ghosts." Boyd nodded, but he still looked confused. Slocum felt too tired to try to explain. "Take my word for it," he finally said, "all I want is a new trail to follow. A warm fire. Sometimes a willing woman. Simple things, that other people don't want bad enough to try and take away from you."

Boyd nodded again, thinking about what Slocum had said.

"Anyway," Slocum added, "if you really mean all those things you said, then Rachel is just the woman you need."

Boyd sighed deeply and said, "I wish *she* knew that."

"Maybe I'll tell her."

Slocum grinned suddenly and spurred his horse into another run. Boyd was still yelling at him as they passed the main body of riders, and he stopped only a few seconds before they reined up in front of Rachel, Boyd eyeing Slocum nervously and Slocum trying not to laugh.

"More excitement?" Rachel asked, looking curiously from one man to the other. "Do you have something new to report?"

Slocum glanced at Boyd, still wanting to laugh at the look of misery on his face. Then he realized that the redhead was really suffering. "No," Slocum said seriously. "The people of Stonetown are probably only figuring it out right about now that no one's on the hill. Even if they find a stray horse or two up in the arroyos . . . well, we'll be halfway to Mesilla and I doubt they'll have the heart to follow."

"Good," said Rachel. "I like taking care of one thing at a time."

The Rancho de Plata crew pushed itself hard, riding on through the morning as the sun got higher and hotter, expecting by mid-afternoon to see a dust cloud on the horizon at any minute.

But the dust cloud never appeared and pretty soon it was obvious that the rustlers had pushed the cattle just as hard, perhaps even driving them by night as well as by day. Rachel Anderson began to wear a constant frown as she scanned the horizon, worrying aloud that the stolen cattle might be lost forever if they were allowed to mix in with other cattle corralled at Mesilla. Slocum kept reminding her that there had been no branding fires, as she herself had mentioned, but Rachel refused to believe it could be that easy. It was Boyd who finally pointed out that three or four hundred cattle couldn't walk into that small a town without being noticed.

"You're right!" Rachel said, suddenly cheerful. "A herd that size doesn't just vanish."

"Of course not. We'll find 'em no matter what brand they're wearing, and make sure they stick around for a brand inspector if we have to."

"Can we, though?"

The red-haired man glanced around at the other riders picking their way through the sage, then showed Rachel a confident smile. "With this bunch we can do anything *you* want done, Miss Anderson."

The woman held his gaze with a bright look of interest, almost as if she had just now become aware of him. "Thank you," she said. "I'll keep that in mind."

In the end it turned out to be easier than anyone had expected, and much more ticklish. The trail led them straight to the banks of the Rio Grande, where the Lazy K riders passed through the shade beneath the cottonwoods and splashed across the shallow river toward the stretch of high ground for which Mesilla had been named. The town was a collection of brown adobe boxes scattered here and there beneath more spreading cottonwoods, but the riders found the cows immediately. They were being herded into a string of railroad cars on a siding at the edge of town. Rachel stopped her big grulla on the far side of the holding pens, staring hard at the cattle just beyond the fence rails and then at the steady activity raising clouds of dust around the cars on the siding. Slocum and Boyd and the rest of the ranch crew waited for instructions, watching her almost comical reaction to the scene before them.

"Am I dreaming?" she asked aloud. "Those are Lazy K brands I see in the pens, aren't they?"

Slocum glanced at the cattle again, although he'd already noticed the letter "K" burned into the animals' flanks. The letter was lying on its side—or on its back, as a lazy letter might.

"Clear as day," he finally said, just to fill the silence.

"And they're openly being loaded in those boxcars."

"Just like they had a bill of sale," said Slocum.

His last words were nearly drowned out by two blasts of a steam whistle, and a few seconds later a small switching locomotive appeared from behind several adobe buildings. The engine was backing slowly down the siding.

"Looks like those beeves might even be goin' out tonight," Boyd said.

"The hell they are!" Rachel snapped, wheeling her horse.

The rest of the crew followed her around the pens. The blond girl trailed along behind, looking uncertain, but Slocum noticed the way she watched every move that Rachel made. It made him think of the way a young boy looked at a vaquero or a gunfighter—whoever his hero happened to be—and it gave Slocum the germ of an idea, which he tucked away in his mind.

There were four rough-looking men on horseback working the cattle out of the pens, hazing them up to a loading chute where a man who wore a brown coat was counting them and making tally marks in a small ledger. The tallyman glanced up when the switching engine coupled into the string of cars, knocking them all back an inch or two, and that was when he noticed the Lazy

K riders coming toward him. They looked weary and their clothes were almost white with trail dust, but they rode with an obvious tension. The tallyman knew from twenty yards away that they were on the prod. He made another mark in his book and then waved his hands and the book above the chute, driving back the uncounted cattle. He also signalled the men in the corral, who eased back and watched the riders pull up in front of the tallyman.

"You're in charge here?" Rachel asked him tightly.

"These are my animals, yes."

"No they're not, mister. You're loading stolen cattle."

The buyer's face lost all expression. "Are you calling me a thief?" he said coldly. "Who do you think you are?"

"My name's Rachel Anderson and my father owns the Lazy K, and I'm telling you that these are stolen cattle."

The buyer began to reach inside his suit coat. Before his hand was even fully concealed he was looking down the bore of Slocum's Colt. From his position slightly off to one side, not directly involved in the confrontation, Slocum had had the time to observe the hard set to the tallyman's face, and the cold gleam in his eye. Slocum had a feeling the man could be dangerous—and he didn't think Rachel was making things any easier by the way she was handling him.

The buyer froze, like a statue with its lips moving. "I'm going to open my coat with my left hand," he said slowly. "You will see that I wear my gun on my hip, not on my shoulder. You will also see a bill of sale in my pocket."

"A bill of sale!" Rachel said. "It can't be."

Slocum was watching the man carefully extract a rumpled piece of paper from his inside coat pocket, exposed now that he was holding the coat away from his body. There was a small pistol tucked away on his hip, just as he had said. Their eyes met and held. Slocum dropped his gun back in its holster, but neither man wanted it to appear that he was backing down. The buyer finally had to look at Rachel as he passed her the paper.

"Three hundred and fifty cows, calves, and yearlings," Rachel read off the paper, a stricken look in her eyes. There was a tense silence while everyone around the woman waited for her to continue, but she just stared numbly at the paper as if she was afraid to look at them.

"Yeah, but is it signed?" Boyd finally asked.

Rachel nodded.

"Then it has to be a fake, Miss Anderson. Your father hasn't even—"

"My brother," the woman whispered, her voice catching. "It's Kevin's signature."

"Kevin!" said Boyd. "You're sure it's his writing?"

Rachel nodded again, her eyes still on the paper, unaware of the look of understanding that passed between Slocum and Boyd. Neither man was surprised, although Boyd was wearing an angry scowl.

"I hope you've learned something," the buyer said, as if he were talking to a child. He reached up to retrieve his bill of sale from the woman's limp fingers. "It's not wise to ride up and start accusing a man before you know all the facts, miss, even if a woman might expect to receive special treatment. People have been shot for much smaller offenses."

If the buyer was expecting Rachel to be contrite, he was disappointed. She drew herself up in the saddle as he spoke and her dark brown eyes became as cold as his. "I wouldn't talk about wisdom," she said. "You're the one holding a worthless piece of paper in your hands. My brother doesn't have any authority to sell Lazy K cows. As far as I'm concerned they're still ours, and I'm taking them back."

The woman started her horse up the chute but the buyer nodded toward the pens at the same time that his hand was sweeping up toward his hip. Slocum had been watching him closely and now he yelled "Watch out!" as he pulled his Colt once more. The men in the corrals were drawing revolvers or sliding rifles out of their saddle boots. Boyd, Rachel, and Chavez had also slapped leather instinctively as soon as Slocum shouted, whirling in their saddles to face the pens. The other vaqueros were slower to react, and decided to make no moves at all when they heard the distinctive and ominous rattle of ten weapons being cocked.

"You're dead!" Slocum barked, holding his Navy square on the buyer. "If I so much as hear a twig snap, you're the first to go."

"Neither one of us wants a bloodbath, you fool. But I can't let you take those animals."

"They're ours to take," Rachel said defiantly.

"So you say, miss. But I've paid for them—paid well—and I have a bill of sale to prove it."

"I told you, my brother doesn't have that authority."

"No?" said the buyer, showing a thin smile. "Then what gives you the authority to take them back?"

Rachel looked confused for a moment, glancing around at the levelled guns gleaming in the late afternoon sun. "Because these cattle have been disappearing from our ranch all year," she said. "We reported them to the sheriff. My father never had any reason to sell them."

"You're sure of that, then? Your father consults you on every decision he makes?"

"Well, not exactly," Rachel faltered. "But I know what he—"

"I repeat," said the man, "I have here a bill of sale signed by the owner's son, and a sizable bank draft is being carried to his representative even as we speak."

"I'll see that your money is returned," Rachel suggested.

The tallyman shook his head. "I need the cows more than I need the money. If I don't fill my contract the way I promised"—his eyes narrowed with a new thought—"well, my reputation wouldn't be the only one to suffer. I'd have to explain it was the Rancho de Plata that reneged on the deal."

"But—"

"I don't know who exactly's to blame, miss. I guess that's your problem. But the deal's been made, and if you break it then the other buyers would be likely to have second thoughts about making deals with your family."

Rachel opened her mouth and then closed it again without saying anything, her pistol drifting an inch or two lower. Slocum took his first full breath, knowing it was over but waiting to see how it would end. Mitch Boyd seemed to understand the problem most clearly.

"I guess it comes down to a question of honorin' a family obligation," he said easily, offering Rachel a way out that would also allow her to save some face. "You ain't even gonna miss three hundred and fifty head, Miss Anderson. And besides, it might be good to give the range a rest this summer. They say it's gonna be a dry one."

"They do, don't they," Rachel agreed, giving Boyd a grateful look.

"You bet. Which means there won't be near 'nough graze, and pretty soon all the ranches hereabouts will be tryin' to sell off their stock. Prices'll go way down, and you'll probably make a nice profit when you replace these critters."

Rachel was still watching Boyd, the tallyman forgotten for the moment, a slow smile spreading across her face. "You have it all figured out?"

Boyd looked at the ground and shrugged. "It just come to me, miss."

He didn't see the woman give him an approving nod

before she turned back to the cattle buyer, taking on an air of dignity that gave Slocum a warm glow of pleasure. "I was hasty," she told the buyer. "I acted out of frustration and anger, and I hope you can forgive me."

"Of course," he said, somewhat diffident at first as he put his gun back on his hip. Then he showed her a gracious smile, although his eyes remained cool and appraising. "I can well understand that communications sometimes break down among family members. I'm only sorry that you've had a long and difficult ride for nothing. Perhaps," he continued, speaking only to the woman, "you would consent to join me for dinner this evening?"

Rachel retained her dignity and her diffidence. "Thank you," she said, "but I'm afraid our ride isn't over yet."

"No?" said the buyer, somewhat startled.

"I mean to find that bank draft," she said grimly, "just to make sure it gets into the right hands. I would very much appreciate your telling me to whom you gave it."

"I don't see why not," said the buyer, looking puzzled. "I just turned it over to one of the men who drove the cattle in."

"The same man you got the bill of sale from?" Slocum asked.

"Yes, as a matter of fact."

Rachel flashed him a startled look. "How could—"

"A wiry little character?" Slocum pressed on. "Long blond hair? Calls himself Riley?"

"Yeah. That's him. He said he'd be taking it up to Chandlerville tonight."

Slocum nodded. "And you said the draft was being delivered, not to Kevin Anderson, but to his *representative*. I believe that's the word you used."

"That's correct. I made out the draft in his name."

"Whose name?" Rachel demanded.

"I'm not sure, now. I'd have to check my—"

Slocum rode his horse in close to the buyer, almost pressing the animal's shoulder into the man's face. "The name?" he said insistently.

"Well . . . I think it was Paulson. Steve Paulson, perhaps?"

Slocum glanced over at Rachel, who nodded slowly. "It could be," she said. "He's a businessman in Chandlerville. Owns a saloon and probably a few other things."

"Tell me something," Slocum said to the buyer, moving his restless horse a couple of inches closer. "Is that a normal way of doing business?"

"Well, I don't usually—"

"Don't you usually buy a man's cattle right from the man himself, face to face? And give him a check in his own name?"

"Usually. But—"

Slocum nudged his horse even closer. "Did those men who brought the cattle really look like vaqueros?"

"I don't know what—"

"You knew this was a smelly deal right from the start, didn't you?" Slocum was looking down at the top of the buyer's head. "Is this how much you value your reputation?"

"Are you calling me a—"

"You're damn right I am!" said Slocum. "What are you going to do about it?"

The buyer reared back with a wild look in his eyes, but he stayed cool enough to remember Slocum's draw a few minutes before. His chest was rising and falling with anger as well as fear, his breath whistling through his nose. The man's body seemed to tremble with his effort to control himself. "You'll see what I do about it," he finally said. "I'll choose the time and place, and then you'll see."

"That's what I thought," Slocum sneered. "A thief's

accomplice and a backshooter, too." He deliberately turned his horse and began riding away, daring the man to take his chance. But a second went by, and then another, and then the rest of the Lazy K riders were falling in behind him, riding warily, half-turned in their saddles with their hands resting on their gun butts. The buyer and his men watched them go, never moving a muscle but also never taking their eyes off the Lazy K crew until they were out of sight.

Boyd eased his horse up beside Slocum's and leaned toward him, the trace of a grin on his lips. "Showing off a little?" he murmured.

Slocum grinned. "Listen to the man who's talking like he already owns the Lazy K ranch!" he said.

13

Slocum escorted Rachel Anderson and Jesus Guttierez into Chandlerville's dusty streets shortly before midnight. The Mexican's hands were still tied behind him and the length of rawhide was still running beneath his horse from one ankle to the other. All three of them were sagging limply as they rode, numb with exhaustion, but they went straight to Steve Paulson's Buckhorn Saloon, where Slocum hitched their horses out front and cut the line that held Guttierez in the saddle.

The horses, at least, were fresher than their riders. Rachel had exchanged mounts for everyone in the crew at a livery in Mesilla, just before she split them up. "I think two of us can handle a saloon owner," she had said with a smile, just before getting serious again. "The thing I'm concerned about now is the folks from Stonetown, and what might happen if they start brooding about the way we treated them this morning."

Boyd had agreed it was a good idea for the vaqueros to get back to the range, but he looked unhappy when he realized Slocum was being chosen to accompany Rachel and the traitor while he himself was being sent back with the riders. He brightened up a little when Rachel made it clear that he would act as her segundo, with her absolute confidence. "You might swing by the canyon," she had suggested. "Look for any sign that it's been used today. Then patrol the spread, check the water holes . . . whatever you think is wise."

"Yes, ma'am," Boyd had answered sharply, followed by an embarrassed glance at Slocum.

"Don't worry," Slocum said, "I'll make sure the boss gets back to you safe and sound."

"Good Lord!" Rachel had said with a sudden laugh. "I'm not your . . ."

A silence fell as her voice trailed off, everyone aware of the strange expression on her face.

"It's your orders we're following," Boyd had said quietly, inspiring a murmured chorus of agreement. "We already made that choice yesterday."

"I hadn't really thought about it like that," Rachel said, tears springing to her eyes. "I don't know how to thank you for . . . for that kind of loyalty." She laughed again, blinking her eyes hard this time. "Now I'll ruin everything by crying. That's not the way a boss should act."

Slocum had raised the problem of Julie, who wouldn't feel safe remaining by herself so close to the outlaws she had run away from. At this suggestion Rachel told the soft-looking Anglo to take the girl back to the ranch and give her a room in the main house, and stay close by to keep an eye on her.

There had still been four men left to go with Boyd, and Slocum could see that they were men who would stick by the segundo and account well for themselves if it came to a fight. Thinking about it made Slocum feel a lot easier now as he helped Guttierez down off his horse.

"Tell me something," he said to the Mexican. "I want to know about that bill of sale before we go inside."

"I don't know anything about a—"

Slocum grabbed the skinny man by his shirt collar and lifted him off the ground with one arm. "You're looking right at a conspiracy charge," Slocum hissed. "Conspiracy in rustling cattle. You'll be lucky if they don't hang you."

"Hang me!" the man squeaked, his eyes bulging with a pitiful fear. "But you heard the man who buy the cattle. You know I only obey the *señor*."

"Kevin?"

"*Sí* . . . Mr. Anderson. He tell me what to do. How can I say no?"

"You could have told my father," Rachel said.

Guttierez bowed his head, and Slocum felt sorry for him. "I know," said the man. "I am ashamed. But more than that, I am afraid of heem."

"I can understand that," Slocum said, glancing at Rachel. "Is that why you didn't mention him when Miss Anderson took you to Stonetown?"

Guttierez nodded. "I am afraid of that man," he said quietly, almost apologetically. "He can be cruel. I have seen it."

Rachel sighed bleakly, looking toward the open door of the saloon. "I'm not sure I can go through with this," she said softly. "I have no idea where it'll end . . . and it could destroy my father."

"What if he finds out anyway? After Kevin does even more damage?"

Rachel continued staring through the door into the yellow glow of coal-oil lamps.

"Let's at least get all the facts," Slocum suggested gently. "You can always decide later what to tell your father, once you know what there is to tell."

"You're right, of course," she said, turning to meet his gaze with a smile. "Are you always right about everything, Mr. Slocum? Because I'm not sure I could stand it for very long."

Slocum took a deep breath and let it out slowly. "You won't have to, Rachel."

"What?"

"I was just passing through to begin with, looking for a bed and a meal. I haven't changed my plans."

Rachel glanced at the Mexican, who was staring hard

at the ground with his head and shoulders nearly hidden by his hat. "But I thought—"

"I know," said Slocum. "Maybe I misled you. Anyway, we never exactly had a chance to talk it out." He watched the look of surprise fade from her face, replaced once again by an expression of bleak hopelessness. "Christ!" he said suddenly. "If only I was a different kind of man."

"What does that mean?"

Slocum looked away, down the street, feeling as if some beast had gripped his chest in its great paw. "When I ride out," he finally said, "I don't think I'll ever come across anyone like you again. Anyone who's got your beauty, your intelligence . . . your spirit."

Rachel averted her eyes with a nice modesty, then managed a faint smile. "But you plan to keep looking anyway?" she said.

"That's the *point*," Slocum said, almost fiercely. "I'm not looking to settle in with anyone. If I were, you'd never be able to get rid of me. And Mitch Boyd would just have to play second fiddle."

"Mr. Boyd?" said Rachel. "What's he got to do with this?"

Slocum smiled. "You can't be that blind. And I'll tell you, Rachel, if I was in your shoes, he'd be my first choice."

The woman's face showed a series of emotions, beginning with annoyance and moving on through curiosity, pleasure, and finally anticipation. Then it seemed to close shut. "But maybe you have the right idea," she said in the end. "It's a lot easier just taking care of yourself."

"Easier?" said Slocum. "I don't know about that. I can tell you it's a hell of a lot lonelier. But you're forgetting something you have that I don't."

"What are you—oh, the ranch?"

Slocum nodded. "I suppose there's a chance that

Kevin will marry someday and decide he wants to come back—if you let him. But what if he doesn't? Who carries on, after you're gone?"

Rachel was gnawing at the inside of her lip, thinking about it. "You have a point," she said, then laughed suddenly and pushed him lightly on the chest. "As usual. Can't you be wrong about something, just once? Just to pretend you're like the rest of us?"

Slocum smiled at her, but his smile turned sickly as a series of bright images flashed in front of his eyes. He could see himself standing over the bodies of a Reconstruction judge and his hired gun. See himself setting fire to the farm his family had worked all their lives to build. See himself riding away, never to return. The pictures all came at once, leaving him with a hollow feeling in his belly.

"Don't worry," he told Rachel, "I already took care of that. I made a mistake big enough for a lifetime."

Rachel tilted her head to one side, giving Slocum a sympathetic look and waiting to hear his story, but in that moment he became aware of Guttierez standing off to one side, still studying the toes of his boots with furious attention.

"Let's give Jesus a break," Slocum said. "I don't think the poor man has moved a muscle in five minutes. We may have already killed him with embarrassment."

A lively gleam of amusement came into Rachel's sharp eyes, animating her face, and Slocum thought she looked more beautiful than he had ever seen her. For just a second he wanted to take back everything he'd just finished saying. But there was already a look of grim determination settling over her features.

"You're right one more time," she said. "Let's go find Steve Paulson."

Slocum took hold of the Mexican's arm and led him around the horses toward the saloon, but stopped a few feet short of the open door. Only then did Guttierez raise his head, to find out what was going on.

"I almost forgot about the bill of sale," Slocum said.

"Is it really important?" asked Rachel.

"I don't know about important, but it might help fill out the picture. The more we figure out, the less they can put over on us."

"What's left to figure out, Slocum? My brother was using a bunch of outlaws to sell some of our father's cattle, and that's the hard, simple truth. I'd be curious to find out why, but other than that..." She ended the thought with a hopeless shrug, weighed down once more by the burden of her brother's behavior and worrying over her father's reaction.

Slocum dropped the Mexican's arm and took Rachel's, walking her toward the corner of the building. "Suppose Kevin claims the paper is a phony?" he asked in a low tone. "Claims he never saw it before. Or what if he says the outlaws forced him to write it? There's also Mr. Paulson to think about. If he doesn't like the smell of things he might pretend he has no idea why the draft is in his name. He might even—"

Rachel held up her hand. "All right," she said wearily, "I see your point. Ask your questions."

Slocum gave her arm a squeeze that was meant to be reassuring and turned back to Guttierez. "You work for the lady now. You realize that, don't you?"

"*Sí! Sí.*"

"You want to help her?"

The Mexican nodded energetically.

"Then tell me. Kevin gave you that bill of sale the day before yesterday, didn't he? When he sent you up on the ridge?"

"Tha's right!" said Guttierez, giving Slocum a curious look.

"The paper was badly crumpled," Slocum explained. "It had been folded many times, and you could see where the ink had run when it was soaked with sweat. It was obvious the rustlers brought it with them on their hard ride, and I could think of only one way it might go from Kevin to them."

"An' you were right, *señor*."

"Then Kevin gave you instructions to warn the rustlers of our approach? And make sure one of them hit you on the head?"

The Mexican nodded, feeling the bump with his hand.

"He had you tell them it was time to take the cows to market?" Slocum pressed.

"I theenk it wass plan' long ago. But yes, I tell them."

"And they were to have the buyer pay the money over to Mr. Paulson?"

"That wass also plan' long time."

"Do you know why?"

Guttierez shook his head.

"But Mr. Anderson was definitely in charge?" Slocum said.

"Oh yes! These others, they not really bad men. They work for *Señor* Anderson."

"You were the one who took them messages from Kevin? Told them when and where to pick up the cattle they were stealing?"

The Mexican nodded. "I would ride at night, sometime."

Slocum looked at Rachel, who stared back with a blank look, then he shrugged and said, "Thank you, Jesus. Why don't you wait for us out here."

"But I don't understand," Rachel said plaintively, showing the wear of a hundred miles in the saddle with only a few hours of sleep on rocky ground. "Why would Kevin need all that money? Why would he steal from his own inheritance?"

Slocum glanced at the saloon. "Let's ask Mr. Paulson," he said.

Rachel closed her eyes, almost visibly drawing on

her well of strength. When she opened her eyes again, the glean of humor had returned.

"Correct me if I'm wrong," she said, "but didn't I just suggest that?"

The Buckhorn Saloon was jammed with boisterous men who, at midnight, had all been drinking steadily for some time. A few of them were somber drunks but the majority were laughing and yelling at each other loud enough to be heard over the noise of everyone else who was also trying to be heard. The sharp crack of billiard balls echoed through the confusion from the back of the big room, and Slocum could see several card games were scattered among the tables. He took his time surveying the crowd, squinting his eyes against the heavy pall of smoke that turned the air grey, but he saw no familiar faces to concern him.

What he did see was the effect Rachel Anderson could have on a bunch of rough and drunken men. Her entrance was treated as one of the major events of the night. Heads turned. Eyes winked. Shoulders straightened. But all of it was lost on the woman, who marched straight to the bar and asked to speak with Steve Paulson.

The bartender was pouring a shot of whiskey for one of the men at the bar. Slocum licked his lips, finding it almost impossible to take his eyes off the whiskey bottle. The bartender took his time, prolonging the agony. He recorked the bottle and put it back on its shelf before he turned to Rachel.

"He's in back," said the bartender, glancing at Slocum and then returning his attention to Rachel. "He might be busy right now. Who should I say wants to see him?"

"Tell him it's Kevin Anderson's sister," she said. "Tell him it's important. He'll probably understand the rest."

The bartender nodded, gave Slocum another thoughtful look, then turned away without a word. They watched him disappear through a black curtain to the right of the bar, and Slocum instinctively thought about the layout of the building. It was the instinct of self-preservation, a built-in awareness of all that went on around him. Automatically he decided that the wall behind the bar was not the outside wall, but an inside core. It probably split the 'dobe in half, with Paulson's office and storerooms and probably other kinds of rooms in back. Slocum arrived at his conclusion, and then forgot about it.

The bartender appeared after a minute or so and held the curtain aside, gesturing to Slocum and Rachel with his other hand. "First door on the right," he said as they went by him into the dimly lit hallway.

Rachel knocked on the door and opened it after a voice told her to enter. Slocum followed her in and closed the door behind him, putting his back to the wall beside it while the woman advanced toward the paper-littered desk in the middle of the room. The man sitting behind the desk had a smooth face, hollow in the cheeks, with glossy black hair that shone in the light from the coal-oil lamp sitting on his desk. Watching from the shadows beyond the desk, Slocum also noticed the way the light caught Paulson's eyes. They gleamed as black as obsidian, the saloon owner watching Rachel with a look of diffident curiosity.

And something about him seemed wrong.

Slocum tried to figure out what it was. To all appearances the man was flawlessly well-groomed. Then Slocum realized he had felt the sting of dust in his nose when he first came into the room. It wasn't a smell that belonged with the immaculate saloon owner, and that was what had alerted Slocum. After a moment's thought he was willing to assume it was only the dust he and Rachel were bringing with them, but he still didn't feel any better about Steve Paulson.

"I'm not sure that you have any business here," he was telling Rachel in a smooth voice. "If in fact your brother and I have any arrangements, then they would be strictly between him and me."

"Of course, Mr. Paulson, except for one thing. It's not Kevin's money."

"No?" said Paulson, arching an elegant black eyebrow. "The cows did belong to your family, did they not?"

Rachel shook her head. "To my father, sir. There's a big difference."

"Oh, come now! Kevin has been working the place with your father for... what? Twenty-five years? Thirty? Don't you think that entitles him to something?"

"Well, of course," Rachel faltered. "In a way he does have part of the Lazy K, but it's an inheritance. It's not his to sell off whenever he wants."

"What else does he have to show, then, for all those years of labor?"

"The ranch itself, damn you!"

Paulson's eyes glinted more sharply and his hollow face became stiff. "What if the ranch itself means nothing to him?" he snapped. "Was it his choice that the old man wanted to run cattle?"

Rachel didn't say anything immediately, and even watching from behind Slocum somehow knew that the thought troubled her. He could imagine the look of pain in her eyes.

Paulson seemed to enjoy it. He smiled a cold smile and opened a box on his desk, extracting a thin black cheroot and placing it between equally thin lips. Slocum watched him light it, lean back in his chair, and blow smoke toward the ceiling. For Slocum it was like watching the bartender pour a glass of whiskey.

"Don't you call him an old man," Rachel suddenly flared. "He's still worth ten men like you. And if Kevin wants to do something else, he's certainly welcome."

"With what?" said Paulson, the smile stretching into an evil grin. "A few dollars a month, that he has to spend on equipment anyway? Your old man holds all the strings."

"Don't call—"

"Either Kevin has to grow up in the old man's image, or he's out the door and on his own." Paulson was sneering at her now. "Oh, yeah, there's only one way to prove himself to the *old man*, and that's to be just like him."

"You have no right—"

"Well, Kevin finally decided he was going to make his own success in his own way, and I say more power to him."

Rachel slumped into a chair, apparently defeated. "How?" she asked in a hushed voice. "What is he planning?"

Paulson tilted his head back and blew another cloud of smoke in the air, then looked at Rachel with something that might have been pity but was more likely an enjoyment of his own superiority, his own power. "We're partners," he said smugly. "As of tonight we're in the hotel business together. You won't spill the beans, because it would ruin him as much as it would ruin me."

"You're buying a hotel?" Rachel whispered.

"Building one!" Paulson said grandly. "We've already taken an option on the site. It'll be just across the street from the depot, once the railroad goes through. We'll have the jump on everyone else. And one day your brother will be a very rich and important man."

"My brother," Rachel repeated, trying to imagine it.

"Maybe then your father will be proud of him," said Paulson. "If he isn't too damn stubborn, he'll see the things that Kevin can accomplish in his own way. Kevin was never meant to be a cattleman."

Slocum knew that here, at least, Paulson was telling the truth. Rachel probably knew it too. She was staring at the top of Paulson's desk. Slocum and the saloon owner both watched her, aware of the raucous sounds drifting in from the main room. The saloon owner decided to press his advantage.

"How do you think your father got *his* start?" he said reasonably. "He began with nothing, too, but he came into this country and rounded up a bunch of cattle that weren't his—"

"They were strays," Rachel murmured. "All mavericks, with no brands."

"Well, they still weren't his to begin with. And neither was the land. He just claimed the water holes and held them with brute force, and that made everything else worthless. You got to fight for what you want, and that's all Kevin did."

"No," said Rachel, sitting up, her tone harder now. "No, he stole."

"From what, his own inheritance? It would have been his anyway—even if it wasn't already, just from putting in years of hard labor."

"He could have asked my father for a loan."

Paulson laughed out loud. "To build a hotel? What do you think your father would have said?"

"I don't care," Rachel said defiantly. "He stole from my father—from all of us together—and he knew he was stealing just from the way he went about it."

"What choice did the old man give him?" Paulson demanded.

Rachel Anderson stood up, her shoulders thrown back, looking more like her father than ever. She was no longer willing to give ground. "That's not the point, Mr. Paulson. The only relevant fact is that the proceeds from the sale of those cows belongs to the Lazy K. Will you sign the draft over to me? Or will I have to resort to legal action?"

The saloon owner looked startled, then alarmed. "You can't do that!" he said. "You'll destroy everything."

"It isn't his money," Rachel insisted.

"But you don't understand. The option runs out to-morrow and we'll lose everything if we don't pay up. Not just the option money, but all our planning. We tipped our hand and now there'll be others to snap it up."

"That's a shame, Mr. Paulson, but it doesn't change the fact you were planning to use stolen money."

"That's just your interpretation," Paulson said desperately.

"I'm sure the courts will see it the same way."

"Think of your brother, then. I'll still be comfortable with my saloon, among other things, but your brother will be left with nothing."

"As he well deserves," Rachel said harshly. "Will you give me the draft, or do I ask for a court order in the morning?"

Paulson stared up at the woman and saw what Slocum couldn't help seeing: an inflexible, unbending woman. The saloon owner seemed dazed. He sighed deeply, frowning, and reached toward his cigar box on the table.

Slocum was worrying about Rachel's inflexibility—wishing she could learn to accept some of the world's imperfections—and so awareness came a fraction of a second too late. He saw Paulson reaching for the box even though a cheroot still dangled from his lips. He remembered the smell of dust in the room and the delay before the bartender had reappeared to point the way through the curtain. He yelled something, his heart seeming to leap inside his chest as his hand whipped down toward the Colt Navy, but he'd only touched the ivory grips when he saw the little double-bored derringer in Paulson's hand. It was pointed straight at Rachel's breast.

"Good," said the saloon owner, glancing at Slocum. "Just leave it on your hip and don't do anything stupid."

The door to Slocum's right opened a moment later and three dust-covered riders crowded into the little room, pistols drawn. One was short and wiry with straggly blond hair. The second was Slocum's size, with brown hair and big ears. The third was short and fat.

"Hello, Riley," Slocum said. "Smith. Coco. I take it you'd just rode in yourselves when the bartender brought word we were here?"

They glared back at Slocum without answering, taking positions around the room.

"You'll have to learn," Paulson was telling Rachel. "Attack isn't always the best choice. There are times when it's smart to retreat, to compromise. Sometimes you just have to admit defeat."

"I agree," Rachel said coldly. "I think that's exactly what you should do."

Paulson laughed. "What *I* should do?"

"Yes. Give me that draft and let the option go, and be content with your saloon while you still have the choice."

Paulson glanced at the gunmen and laughed again, with a little less certainty. "You don't seem to realize you're at somewhat of a disadvantage here."

"Am I?" the woman said, glancing disdainfully at the outlaws. "Do you really want to pit these miserable thieves against my father and the Lazy K riders? And Sheriff Wingfield? That I'd like to see."

"You may not be around," Paulson snapped.

"Don't be stupid, you weasel. The whole crew knows where we came and why. The most you can hope for is to buy enough time to invest that money. Then we'll just have the judge turn it over to the Lazy K."

The saloon owner kept his cold black eyes on the woman's face for a few seconds, then leaned back in his chair and motioned with the derringer. "Get them out of here," he said to the outlaws.

"Do we kill 'em?" Riley said hopefully.

"No! Not yet, anyway." Paulson was staring moodily at the top of his desk. "God damn it, just get them the hell out of town long enough for me to think."

14

The short Mexican called Coco checked the dark hallway, then motioned Slocum and Rachel to follow him toward the back door, Smith and Riley bringing up the rear. The one named Smith lifted Slocum's Colt out of its holster and used it to prod him roughly out the door and through the black shadows of a deserted alley behind the saloon.

"Are you boys real bandits?" Slocum taunted. "Or do you always have to get help from the people you're robbing?"

The muzzle of his revolver was jammed into his back, just above the kidney. The front sight of the gun sliced a hole in his shirt and skin. Slocum cursed and jerked away from the blow, but a nasty smile appeared on his face.

"Because if you do," he said, "I don't see how you can make it in the business. Most folks aren't so cooperative."

The pistol struck again, shoving him forward with the blow. Slocum had to make a great effort not to reach for the gun. He might have tried it if he'd been alone, grabbing for the weapon when he expected the blow, then taking advantage of its momentum to yank it through and under his shoulder, trying to aim it toward Coco walking in front. Smith would either pull the trigger, shooting down one of his own partners, or else

152

Slocum would twist the gun out of his hand and . . . well, he couldn't have planned it beyond that. It would depend on how fast the bandits reacted. He'd have pulled the trigger himself, or lashed out with the gun, or used whatever combination seemed appropriate. He badly wanted to give them a taste of the terrifying speed and ferocity that had done so well for the men under Quantrill.

But Quantrill never had any women along to worry about.

"One more word out of you," a voice was saying behind him, "and we'll forget about Mr. Paulson's orders."

Slocum's scorn for the bandits caused him to open his mouth for another remark, but then he only sighed. There was no point in baiting them if he didn't intend to take advantage of any openings.

And now that he knew he wouldn't, that he was truly trapped once again, he was overcome with an awesome weariness. Two blows on the head, dozens of hours of hard riding, the tension of shooting and being shot at, a day and a night of clawing at baked mud with his fingernails . . . it all came rushing in on him, so that giving up felt like sweet relief. His eyes closed softly as he walked, his arms and legs wobbling as if the bones had fallen out of them. He and Rachel would see where they wound up, and get a good night's rest while they had the chance. Time enough to worry in the morning. Paulson might even be smart enough not to try to bluff it through. He looked smart enough. A greasy son of a bitch, sure, but he hadn't got where he was by being stupid. Slocum hoped they were going somewhere with something soft to sleep on. A mattress was probably too much to hope for, but some loose hay would do.

"Put up the guns, boys. We've got you surrounded."

Slocum blinked, pulling himself out of his waking dream. There was a second of frozen silence, the future balancing on the edge of a razor, with Rachel gripping his arm.

"It's Henry," she whispered excitedly. "The sheriff!"

Slocum found it hard to believe. His instincts hadn't even hinted at the presence of other men around them.

The outlaws were also finding it hard to believe, it seemed. One man might have them covered, that much they could accept. But surrounded? Already? In a dark and remote alley? Slocum tensed, ready to spring.

"Lower those guns *now*," barked an old man's voice, from a more clearly defined direction. "Do it or I start—"

The threat was cut short by the concussion of gunfire crashing in the narrow alley, explosions one on top of another that bounced off adobe walls and pounded the ears. Slocum was already flying through the air. He'd seen the bandits begin their pivot and in the same instant he'd launched himself toward Rachel, circling her in his arms and pulling her to the ground. From there he twisted his head up to see what was happening.

He was surprised to see that Smith and Coco had already joined him in the dirt, while Riley was limping away down the alley. It flashed through Slocum's mind that they must have been surrounded after all. Then he saw a tall, lean figure emerge from the shadows, alone and moving easily toward them, his eyes on the retreating bandit.

Slocum checked the other two again. Coco wasn't moving, except for the boiling bubbles of blood that spurted several inches out of his heaving chest. Smith was writhing in the dirt, but he was slowly bringing Slocum's Navy off the ground, pointing it toward the sheriff.

Slocum struggled to his hands and knees and dove for Smith, grappling with him at the same time he heard Riley fire another shot. From the corner of his eye he could see Wingfield slowly raising his pistol out at arm's length, with never even a hint of flinching.

Slocum twisted his Colt out of Smith's fingers and clubbed him over the head with it. The sheriff was carefully sighting down the barrel of his pistol, two more slugs ripping toward him down the alley. He fired once and smoothly eased back the hammer, acting as if he was in no hurry and yet getting off his second shot as fast as any man Slocum had ever seen. Smith was reaching for Slocum's throat. Slocum clubbed him again, feeling a grim satisfaction when the outlaw groaned and settled to the ground.

The wiry bandit named Riley was also sinking to the ground, about twenty yards down the alley. Slocum squinted at him for a second, seeing no movement in the shadowy little lump, then climbed to his feet and offered Rachel a hand. He glanced over at the sheriff, who had lowered his pistol and was now poking at Smith's body with the toe of his boot.

"Thanks for the help, son," said the old man.

"Mr. Wingfield!" Rachel cried, steadying herself against Slocum. "Thank *you!* You were wonderful. How did you ever know?"

The lean old man gave her an amused look, which also contained something else. "That's the business I'm in. After forty-one years of doin' a thing, a man ought to know a little about doin' it, don't you think?"

"Yes, but..."

Rachel didn't finish her sentence. She couldn't, not without betraying her family's loss of faith in Wingfield's abilities. But she was staring at him with a puzzled expression and he was still looking back at her with that patient, half-amused look, as if he was trying to tell her something without putting it into words.

"Were you really alone?" Slocum asked him, still not fully convinced.

The sheriff nodded, turning his kindly eyes on Slocum. "It seemed easier and quicker than dragging a deputy along."

"Damn!" said Slocum, shaking his head. "I don't

think I've ever seen a prettier piece of shooting."

"Thank you," Wingfield said modestly. "Like I say, forty-one years . . ." His voice trailed off as he peered down the alley. "Come on," he said.

They followed him quietly, Rachel glancing at Slocum with an inquiring tilt of her head and Slocum only shrugging his shoulders in bewilderment. It had almost seemed like magic, the way Wingfield appeared from nowhere to rescue them. He certainly didn't have any explanation to offer.

The sheriff squatted beside Riley's body long enough to make sure the outlaw was dead. Then he stood and began walking back toward the main street. "Come on," he said again. "I better get the undertaker down here."

Rachel and Slocum glanced at each other once more, then hurried to catch up with him.

"You also may be the most uninquisitive sheriff I've ever come across," Slocum told him.

Wingfield smiled. "Not necessarily, son. But there's a time for everything, and everything has its time. Right now I'm concerned with cleaning up those bodies, so they won't offend any sensative young maidens who might be strolling through the alley. We have all night to talk about Mr. Paulson."

"But, Sheriff," Rachel faltered, "if you know about Steve Paulson, let's go see him right now. Before he has an opportunity to dispose of the bank draft."

Wingfield stopped dead. "He actually had a draft?"

"Why, yes. Those rustlers brought it to him tonight."

"That would make sense," the old man murmured, rubbing his chin as he stared at the ground. Gradually he started walking again, still thoughtfully rubbing his chin.

"I don't understand," Rachel said, catching up again with Slocum at her side. "You act as if you're perfectly familiar with a story we've only learned about tonight."

"Tell me your story," said Wingfield.

"Well . . ." Rachel was frowning into the distance, wondering where to begin. "Those three men in the alley, they were the ones who've been stealing our beeves all year. They were collecting them up above Stonetown and today—yesterday—they sold them all in Mesilla. They brought the draft to Mr. Paulson, in his name. But they were only working for Kevin . . . for my brother." Rachel coughed and Slocum could see tears streaming down her cheeks, reflecting the stray lights along the main street of Chandlerville. "My brother," she began, unable to finish the sentence.

"Apparently Kevin made a deal with Steve Paulson," Slocum finished for her. "They're planning to go in on a new hotel together."

"With money he stole from my father!" Rachel cried. "I was trying to get it back when Mr. Paulson had those men take us away. Can't we go get it from him now, Mr. Wingfield? He'd have no choice but to give it to you. Otherwise we could accuse him of . . . of unlawful imprisonment."

Wingfield was walking a little slower now, drifting closer to Slocum and Rachel. "What would you do with the draft?" he asked.

"Give it to my father, of course. Why do you ask?"

"You mean you'd tell him what Kevin has done?"

"Of course," said Rachel, tears giving way to surprise. "I wouldn't have a choice. He ought to know, don't you think?"

"No, I don't," said Wingfield, leaning in suddenly and slipping Slocum's Colt out of his holster. "I'm afraid you two are under arrest."

"For what?" demanded the woman.

The sheriff frowned, stepping away to level Slocum's Colt and then his own at the two of them. "I suppose for assault," he finally said, glancing at Slocum. "That man might have lived if you hadn't bashed him the way you did."

"But he was saving your life!"

"Forget it," Slocum said bitterly. "Don't you see it yet? The reason he could never catch those rustlers? The reason he knew all about the deal?"

"Oh, God," said Rachel, putting her hand to her mouth and falling back to stare at the sheriff with horror. "You and them? Against you oldest friend?"

Wingfield was just standing there, not saying anything, but the more Slocum looked into his face the more he began to question his own interpretation. The sheriff's leathery face remained impassive, yet there seemed to be a deep sadness in his eyes, if Slocum wasn't just kidding himself.

"Please," Rachel said. "Tell me Slocum's wrong."

"I have to think about this," Wingfield mumbled. "Just move along. You know where the jail is, Rachel."

"Oh, God," she said again. "How much was it worth to betray my father? How much are they paying you?"

"Just move, damn it."

Slocum drifted heavily out of a deep and dreamless sleep to the sound of Rachel's voice, and then the sheriff's, one sharp and angry, the other insistent and pleading. That was the word that came to Slocum just before his eyes opened on the steel bars a few inches in front of his face.

The sheriff was pleading with Rachel.

It had to be late morning, Slocum decided, with sunlight pouring in through a high window and splashing across the walls of his cell. He struggled to remember the details of the previous three days—in the canyon, in the adobe, and in the Buckhorn—which all seemed dreamlike and unreal now that he was finally separated from them by a night of rest. He listened to the conversation a moment longer, then sat up to watch. Rachel was on her bunk in another cell and Wingfield was standing at the cell door.

The only one who seemed to notice that Slocum was awake was Jesus Guttierez, who watched from the cell across the aisle.

The sheriff had agreed to find Guttierez, who'd been left waiting outside the Buckhorn Saloon, and put him up for the night in protective custody. Paulson or Kevin Anderson would eventually figure out that the Mexican had switched sides.

"I'm trying to say your father doesn't have to know," the sheriff was telling Rachel. He closed his eyes and sighed deeply, then gave the woman a strange look. "Believe me," he said, in that pleading tone again, "there are a lot of things in this life that we're just better off not knowing."

"That's never been my father's way. He takes things as they come and he makes the best of them."

"Lord, if you ain't exactly like him when he was your age," Wingfield said with great sadness. "But that's just youth talking, Rachel. I've *lived* longer than you, and it just stands to reason I've learned another thing or two."

"Like incompetence? Like playing Judas to your oldest friend?"

Wingfield glared at her, more angry now than sad. "Yep," he said, "the spittin' image of your old man. Always so goddamned sure of himself, so sure he was right about everything."

"You really hate him, don't you?" said Rachel. "That's why you conspired against him. To bring him down to your level."

The sheriff groaned but he also smiled, as if he couldn't help it. "What a fool you are," he said with wistful tolerance. "I don't hate your father. I feel more for him . . . well, I don't hate him." Wingfield coughed and pulled his hat down lower over his eyes. "You'll never even begin to know what's between us, Rachel, and that's exactly why I don't want him told about your brother. It would just hurt him too much to know."

"It hurt him to think you were letting him down," Rachel said coldly. "That you weren't man enough to do your job any more."

Slocum could see that the jab hit home. Wingfield gripped the bars with his bony hands, bowing his head to stare at the floor. "I know," he said quietly. "I had a choice between letting him lose faith in me, and telling him something that would break his heart." The old man nodded to himself. "Well, I made the choice and I'm planning to live with it, Rachel. Doesn't that give you an idea how strong I feel about the things I'm telling you?"

"But why?" said Rachel, finally affected by the sheriff's expression. "Why not just tell him straight out? Did you really think it would stay a secret forever?"

"That's the part I'm asking you to trust me on," Wingfield begged. "I got my reasons, but I don't want to tell you what they are."

"Probably reasons of profit," Rachel said, although her voice lacked conviction now. "That is, if you even knew what was going on to begin with."

Wingfield heard the change in her tone. He met her eyes for a long moment, and then repeated her name again with a long sigh. "Do you really think I could be that ignorant? You can't live in a county and try to enforce its laws for forty-one years without having some idea of what's going on, can you? I been makin' other friends all through that time, Rachel. People who like to talk to an old fart like me. They keep their ear to the ground and pass on what I ought to know, and I put it together."

Rachel watched the sheriff with a brooding look, her lower lip pulled in between her teeth.

"Like noticing the way—just as an example—the way your brother was spending so much time in town," the sheriff said. "Frequenting the Buckhorn and being heard to complain about ranch life, telling Paulson he wished he could have a business of his own. Then later I hear that Paulson has an option on four lots where the railroad's going through. I wonder about that, and decide four lots has to mean something the size of a hotel. Then there's more rumors about the railroad, the option . . . but also the rumors saying that Paulson lives too high. No one believes he could ever put up all the money to build a hotel. And then comes word of losses on the Lazy K."

The sheriff and the rancher's daughter eyed each other through the bars, Rachel beginning to nod slowly at the old man. A freight wagon rattled by in the street outside, and a fly buzzed erratically through a shaft of sunlight.

"Then you suspected all along," Rachel said at last. "You weren't part of it?"

The sheriff shook his head.

"I'm sorry," Rachel said, looking down. "I shouldn't have had to ask that. But still . . . you suspected."

"I *knew,* after a while. I'm like the spider at the center of its web, Rachel. If something lands in the county, I usually know about it."

The woman leaned back on her bunk, frowning thoughtfully. "I want to trust you," she said slowly, "but I just don't understand how it can be kept from my father."

"Believe me, it can."

"But what if Kevin finds more bandits and continues his stealing? Or tries to embezzle funds directly?"

"He won't," Wingfield said tightly.

"You can't be sure, though. He could develop a taste for thievery. His investments could go sour. You *can't* be sure."

"You're assuming you have all the facts before you," Wingfield said gently. "Can't you just trust my judgment?" He grinned. "It's based on seventy-eight years of bein' alive out here."

Rachel answered his smile with one of her own, but

if faded gradually, to be replaced with a look of rigid determination. "I'm truly sorry," she said, "but I'm sure my father will want to know. No matter how it hurts."

Wingfield sighed one last time, looking more miserable than ever. "I guess I knew you'd say that all along," he told her. "You're too rigid, Rachel, too unbending. Just like him. But I have someone else I want you to talk to."

The woman watched with curiosity as Wingfield moved toward the door that separated the cells from the front office of the jail, shuffling along as if he'd just turned into an old man. He opened the door and nodded to someone in the office, then waited until a stout white-haired gentleman with kindly eyes came past him.

"Dr. Shea!" said Rachel, clearly startled.

Slocum looked at the white-haired man, at the way he was looking at Rachel, and suddenly he understood. He pictured the old rancher climbing on his horse and then showing what it had cost him. Rachel understood too, it seemed. She was shrinking back against the cell wall, a frightened look in her eyes.

"It's bad news," the doctor said immediately, sparing her the agony of uncertainty. "Your father only has another month or so. Three at most."

"No!" Rachel cried. "He's just been feeling poorly, that's all. He'll come around."

"No, he won't," the doctor insisted gently, "because he's dying. But he's had a long and rewarding life, Rachel. He takes great pride in the two of you—"

"Which is what I want him to keep," said Wingfield, still standing by the door.

The doctor glanced back at the sheriff, looking annoyed. "Great pride," he repeated. "And he's done much more than most men ever dream of doing, Rachel. He has no real regrets about this, and I hope you won't either when you think about it. I know you'll miss him, but please don't make his last days hard for him. It's the very thing he was afraid of, the reason he decided not to tell anyone." The doctor looked at the sheriff again. "I only hope my betrayal of his wishes proves to be justified."

"Do you understand now?" Wingfield pleaded, his voice a whisper. "Kevin will have the ranch to himself anyway. In just another month or two, what he's doing won't be illegal at all. It'll be his right. Maybe I was wrong, Rachel, but I just couldn't bring myself to ruin the end of Foley's life for something that came so close to not even being a crime."

Rachel nodded slowly, her eyes distant and unfocused. "You were even willing to sacrifice yourself," she said softly. "Your own standing in his eyes."

"Well, sure, Rachel. It was you kids he lived for. Take any part of that away and what would he have left? His whole life wouldn't mean a damn thing to him."

Rachel was still staring off, still nodding, but she seemed to be unaware of the motion. Her entire body began to rock gently on the bunk. The sheriff and the doctor exchanged looks and then continued to watch her, giving her time to accept and understand.

There came the light sound of running in the street outside, followed by the front door of the jailhouse opening and closing. Wingfield glanced through the doorway in which he was standing.

"Sheriff," came a breathless young voice. "He's here!"

Wingfield put a finger to his lips and disappeared into the front office, but the harshly whispered words were still audible.

"I been watchin', just like I promised," the boy said with excitement. "Kevin Anderson rode up to the Buckhorn not more than three minutes ago!"

Everyone heard the sheriff thank the boy, heard the faint clink of small coins, and then the boy went out through the door again.

"I want to see him," Rachel said as soon as Wingfield had returned.

"But, Rachel—" said the doctor.

"Don't worry, I won't tell him." A grim sense of purpose had returned to her expression. "It would be a bad mistake to tell him," she added, "but we have to settle this somehow."

"I don't know," said the sheriff, rubbing his jaw.

"I want to see him," Rachel insisted. "Let me out, please." She glanced at Slocum, who nodded agreement. "Both of us. I have to talk to my brother."

15

A different bartender was on duty when Slocum and Rachel came into the Buckhorn Saloon, blinking their eyes and almost blind at first in the murky light. The night before the Buckhorn had seemed like a warm pool of light in a dark desert night; now the saloon itself seemed like a dark refuge from the burning desert sun.

The bartender was busy with the noon dinner crowd and Slocum and Rachel were able to get halfway across the room before he noticed them. But when he did he moved immediately toward the black curtain in the wall behind the bar.

Slocum pulled the Colt that Wingfield had returned to him and glowered as menacingly as he could, sighting down the barrel at the bartender. "Paulson must have told him what we looked like," he said to Rachel out of the side of his mouth. "The bastard's expecting us." He said it quietly, and he didn't say a word to the bartender, afraid that his voice would carry into Paulson's office. He was aware of the hushed silence descending gradually over the room as the drinkers and diners stopped to stare. He simply had to hope the saloon owner wouldn't notice. In the silence he could hear pieces of an excited but muffled conversation coming through the black curtain.

The bartender had stopped in mid-stride and backed against the wall, his eyes on the gun and going wide with fear. Slocum replaced his scowl with a more friendly look, winking at the bartender and holding his finger to his lips as he went on by with Rachel at his side.

He turned to the rest of the men in the saloon and made an encouraging motion with his pistol, flapping the thumb and fingers of his other hand together. The customers stared dumbly back at him. He moved his lips silently, still making the sign of chatter with his free hand. Here and there the men started to talk again, uncertainly, keeping an eye on Slocum's Colt.

Slocum and Rachel had almost reached the curtain when Slocum stopped and turned back.

"What?" whispered Rachel.

Slocum pointed his pistol at a bottle of whiskey on the bar and then at a glass beside it. Rachel sighed with exaggerated patience while the bartender inched forward to pour a glass, splashing a little whiskey on the bar. He stepped back against the wall again while Slocum drained the glass, squeezing his eyes closed for an instant and thinking nothing had ever tasted as good.

"Courage?" he heard Rachel murmur.

Slocum shook his head. "Thirst!" he said.

"You've earned it, anyway."

Slocum nodded at the bartender, then gave him another warning glance before he followed Rachel through the curtain. Now he was grateful for the silence in the saloon, if not the attention they were getting. He and Rachel were able to hear most of the conversation on the other side of the door.

"The point you're missing," Paulson was saying, "is that it's useless to go ahead with the option because your father could still ruin us in court."

"That's a chance I'm willing to take," said Kevin. "The hell with him, anyway. He can't prove anything."

"Of course he can, you fool. What if the Mexican talks? Guttierez by himself could expose your whole scheme."

"I can take care of him," Kevin said ominously.

"I don't want any part of that stuff, Kevin. I'm not willing to take the same chances you are. Just think what would happen if we pay for the lots and then your father recovers the money."

"He'd have to prove it was his."

"Damn it, Kevin, that's easy enough even without Guttierez. You just finished telling me, your sister and that goddamn drifter already got as far as Harry Waters."

Slocum and Rachel smiled at each other, but for Rachel it was only a half-hearted gesture. Her expression was a mixture of anger and deep sadness as she listened to her brother reveal more and more of his true nature.

"That's what Wilson said when he brought the girl back," Kevin admitted.

"What girl?"

"Some whore Slocum talked to up at Stonetown."

"Jesus Christ!" Paulson groaned. "Another witness. So all they have to do is go find Harry Waters, who would testify in court that he arranged with you to pay me ten thousand dollars, for cattle with a Lazy K brand on them. That's all it would take. As soon as Waters finished telling his story the judge would tell Baca to give the money back."

"He couldn't do that, could he? Why should the judge penalize Baca if he didn't know anything about where the money came from?"

"Damn it, Kevin, I don't know what the judge can do . . . but whatever it is would be bad. *Someone* would have to pay, and I sure don't have that kind of money. Do you? The judge could slap a lien on one of us — or both of us. And even if he just nullified the sale and gave Baca his land back . . . Well, that would be just as much of a disaster for me. No one in this town would ever do business with me again."

"So you're backing out on the deal," Kevin said, an edge in his voice.

Slocum and Rachel exchanged tense looks, sharing the idea that things were quickly going from bad to worse. Slocum rested his hand on the doorknob.

"I'm telling you it's foolish to continue," Paulson said reasonably.

"Shit, you're just running scared."

"That's easy for you to say because I'm the one with the most to lose. I'll tell you what. I'll sign the draft over to you and *you* can buy the lots, in your own name."

"I can't do that. It would be too obvious."

"Now who's running scared?" Paulson sneered. "You just don't give a damn if it's me that's taking the risk."

"For the first time you've got something right," Kevin rasped, his words punctuated by the cocking of a pistol. "You'll take that bank draft to Baca right now, or you'll die. I don't care which."

Slocum twisted the door handle and stepped carefully into Paulson's office, cocking his Colt as soon as both men would be sure to hear it. Kevin was spinning on his heel, bringing his gun around, his face twisting with hatred when he recognized Slocum.

"Don't!" commanded Rachel, coming up beside Slocum.

Kevin hesitated but it was obvious that he was measuring his chances, still deciding, so full of rage that he wanted to try for a shot.

"She's right," Slocum said immediately, nodding toward Paulson's desk. "You're covered from two sides."

The boy snapped his head around to see Paulson's hand obscured behind the upraised lid of a cigar box. While they watched, the saloon owner lifted his hand higher to reveal the derringer it held. "I never would have thought I'd be glad to see you," Paulson told Slocum, with the hint of a smile.

"Don't listen to him," Kevin said, recovering himself. "I was trying to get our money back."

"Shut up," said Rachel.

"But he's been stealing—"

"I told you to shut up!"

Brother and sister glared at each other in a silence that seemed to build over several seconds, with Slocum and Paulson as spectators. Kevin was the first to look away, which was when Rachel turned and carefully shut the door behind her.

"Let's all of us take it easy," Slocum said, sliding Kevin's pistol out of nerveless fingers and stuffing it in his own belt. Paulson wasn't so ready to give up his derringer, flashing Slocum a briefly defiant look before his eyes fixed on the muzzle of the Colt Navy that Slocum was holding less than a foot from his nose.

"I wasn't going to let them hurt you," he said as he gave up his gun.

"You should be more careful about the company you keep," said Slocum.

"But that was Kevin. He—"

"Liar!" shouted Kevin, coming up behind Slocum to lean his massive body over the desk. "It was your idea to—"

Slocum drove his elbow back into Kevin's belly and the young rancher doubled over, gripping the edge of the desk and gasping for air.

"Your sister told you to shut up," Slocum said. "We've been listening long enough to know where you stand—both of you. So why don't you have a seat, Kevin, and let's see what she wants to do about it."

Slocum tucked Paulson's derringer behind his belt next to Kevin's pistol as Kevin stumbled into an overstuffed chair beside the desk, returning Slocum's stare with a sharp, hard look of his own. There had been something between them ever since they first laid eyes on each other, Slocum realized, an instinctive dislike that had only been made worse by Slocum's meddling in Rancho de Plata affairs. Now his meddling had exposed Kevin's scheme on the very day it was scheduled to end in victory. Kevin had worked and plotted for a year, dreaming of a great success that would free him of a life he apparently hated, and just when the dream was in his hands Slocum had appeared from nowhere to snatch it away. Not only destroying the dream, but exposing him before his sister and the men who worked for him. Slocum held Kevin's malignant stare for a long moment, warning himself that this was a man who might have lost everything and who also might be capable of violent hatred.

Slocum backed off to the side of the room to watch, in effect giving Rachel center stage. He glanced at her, wondering what she would do, and grateful that it was her decision. He was expecting a harsh declaration of some kind, a series of rigid demands, but one minute of silence faded into the next.

"I don't know," she finally said, her voice nearly a whisper as she stared at the floor of Paulson's office. She looked up at Slocum. "Any more brilliant ideas?" she asked him.

Slocum hesitated, not wanting to let her down.

"No," she said suddenly. "That's not fair. It's my responsibility." She frowned at him with an ironic expression. "It's just that I can only think of one way to go—everything points to it—and yet it's not *right.*"

Slocum nodded sympathetically, suspecting he knew what she had in mind. "I guess life doesn't always get tied up in neat packages," he said.

"I guess not!" she agreed, looking almost as if she were about to laugh at the joke being played on her. She sighed and turned toward Kevin and Paulson, who both seemed baffled. "I don't want our father to find out," she told them. "It's that simple. We can't get the cattle back anyway, and knowing what kind of skunk Kevin turned out to be . . ." Her voice was full of scorn as she stared at her brother, who refused to meet her eyes. "I just don't want his father to have to know."

"Are you saying—" Paulson began.

"That's right," Rachel said, directing her attention at the saloon owner, *"you're* off the hook. There's nothing else we can do with that ten thousand dollars . . . no way to return it to the Lazy K without my father knowing about it. So you're going to get what you want, namely a half-interest in that hotel. But the other half—"

Kevin looked up hopefully as Rachel faltered.

"Damn!" she said. "I can't even do that. It'll have to show on the books as Mr. Paulson's hotel, or word is sure to get back to my father."

"That's right," Kevin said, still looking a little dazed, but also more eager now that it seemed like he was getting off the hook himself.

"But I don't want you getting your hands on the profits," Rachel said coldly. "You're going to stay on that ranch until our father is gone."

"But that could be—"

"I don't care," Rachel snapped. "I don't care how long he lasts. He's going to die thinking the Lazy K will live on under your care. And your son's after that."

"But, Rachel—"

"That's the deal, Kevin."

Now she was as set and rigid as Slocum had ever seen her. He was thinking to himself: *Good girl!* He was also wondering if someday he might not hate himself for leaving her behind.

"If you don't like the deal," Rachel was saying, "then Mr. Paulson can hand me that bank draft right now."

"Kevin," said the saloon owner, "think about it. We

don't have any choice. I could hold the profits for you
—it might not even be all that long—and you'll be a
rich man when the time comes!"

"How would it work?" Kevin asked Rachel. "How
could we protect ourselves?"

"A contract," she said immediately. "Spell it all out,
with copies for everyone concerned."

"What would it say?"

"That Mr. Paulson is acting in behalf of a partnership
with the Rancho de Plata—"

"The ranch!" Kevin said. "But . . ."

"It can't be in your name," Rachel said. "Then you'd
have legal right to the profits and you'd be free to do
what you wanted. This way the hotel will just be one of
the interests that you inherit along with all the rest."

The young rancher was looking miserable. "You've
thought of everything," he said, as if it was an accusa-
tion. "You just want to see me suffer."

"You're damn right!" Rachel flared. "At least, if it
comes down to a choice between your suffering and our
father's . . . well, there isn't any question in my mind."

"All right," Kevin said with a hopeless shrug. "Let's
draw up the contract. Do we get a lawyer, or—"

The office door burst open suddenly. Slocum came
off the wall, earing back the hammer of his Colt. Foley
Anderson shuffled in with Sheriff Henry Wingfield right
behind him. "You won't need no damn lawyer," the old
rancher said gruffly. "Or the pistol," he added, glancing
at Slocum. "Put that damn thing away."

"Yes, sir," said Slocum.

"Father!" cried Rachel. She glanced over his
shoulder at the sheriff, who only offered her a helpless
shrug of his shoulders.

Kevin was struggling out of the chair with a stricken
look, his mouth hanging open but unable to say anything.

"What Rachel isn't telling you is that I'm dying," the
old man said to his son.

"Dying?" Kevin repeated, his eyes glistening suddenly with tears.

"That's what I said. I guess I should have told you, but I didn't want you to fret and worry. I guess I was trying to protect you. But instead"—he glanced back at Wingfield—"everyone's trying to protect *me*."

"I didn't know, Daddy. I didn't mean—"

"Shut up, Kevin. It's hard for me to even call you my son. You've done a despicable thing."

"Yes, sir, I know, but—"

"I have to take some of the blame, Kevin. Maybe a lot of it, if I didn't raise you right. But most of all I blame myself for turning into a blind old fool, believing what I wanted to believe."

The rancher's son fell back into his chair, a lost look on his face, while Rachel moved a little closer to her father, hesitantly, as if she wanted to touch him but was afraid to. "I'm sorry," she said brokenly, tears streaming freely down her cheeks. "I didn't want you to find out about Kevin."

The old man gave his daughter a sad look, reaching tentatively to touch her arm but then letting his hand fall before he could offer her more comfort. "I know," he said gently. "But it's all right, daughter. Some part of me probably knew all along. And now . . . actually, I'm glad it's come to this."

"Glad?"

He nodded. "It means I've got a chance to set things right before I die. I think it's worked out for the best."

The rancher's words set Slocum's pulse racing. He wondered if either of Anderson's children had begun to contemplate their meaning.

"Kevin," said Foley Anderson.

The boy looked up, his eyes still glazed. "Yes?"

"You go ahead and buy those lots, and build the hotel with Paulson. That'll be your payment for the years you spent with me."

Kevin's eyes were focusing now, as he began to understand what his father was saying. "Payment, sir?"

"That's right. You've suffered because of my blind-ness and it seems only fair. But I don't ever want to see you again."

"Oh, no! You can't mean it."

"You've shamed me, boy. The hands will have orders to throw you off the place if you come around."

"Oh, no," the boy said again, burying his head be-tween his knees and crying openly.

"That's as long as I'm alive," said Anderson. "After I'm gone, it'll be up to Rachel."

Kevin slowly raised his head, studying his father's face. "I don't understand," he said.

"Why not?" the old man snapped. "It's simple enough. From the things I heard this morning—right here, and the things my man Wilson has been telling me about the last few days—it's pretty clear to me that she's the one who can make the ranch what I always wanted it to be."

"No, Father, wait," said Rachel, looking guilty and confused. "I should have told Wilson not to tell you anything."

"Mind's made up," the old man barked. Then he softened, winking at his daughter. "You really think Wilson could hold out on me?" he said. "Besides, it's the only choice I have. And I think it's a damned good one."

Kevin buried his head between his knees again, hug-ging them, while Rachel threw her arms around her fa-ther—no hesitation this time. Slocum turned away, partly to offer a small suggestion of privacy and partly to hide his grin. It didn't feel right, being so happy at such a sad time.

"I want to thank you, Mr. Slocum."

The old rancher had come up to stand next to him, his hand outstretched. Slocum shook it. "Sure," he said, shrugging his shoulders. "One thing just led to another."

"I wish I'd been there to see you walking into Stone-town," said the rancher, a strange light suddenly flickering in his eyes.

"We only walked out thanks to your daughter."

Anderson turned to look at Rachel, but he wasn't really seeing her. His gaze drifted on toward the sheriff, something else entirely occupying his mind. "By God," he told Wingfield, "I think it's high time we put Stone-town out of business, don't you?"

The sheriff looked puzzled. "Well, sure," he said, "but why—"

"We're done with roundup on the Lazy K," Anderson said. "So I don't have anything particular planned for the next couple of days. What about you?"

A slow smile was spreading across Wingfield's face, but mostly Slocum noticed the man's eyes. They were sparkling with a lively fire that seemed to turn the sheriff into a young man again. The same thing was happening to Foley Anderson. It was as if forty years had just peeled away.

"No, Father," said Rachel. "Please . . ."

Kevin was looking dazedly from one man to the other.

"Count me in," Slocum said, stepping away from the wall.

"Sorry," Anderson said shortly. "We don't need you underfoot out there."

"Father, please!" Rachel begged.

"I want to be part of this," Slocum insisted.

"Christ," said Wingfield, "it sounds like you took care of most of them already. Why not let us have a little fun, too?"

"Yeah," Anderson said happily. "There can't be any more than ten or twelve left, can there? We ought to keep it a fair fight."

"This is stupid!" Rachel blazed. "Stop acting like kids."

The sheriff threw back his head and laughed, giving Rachel a fond look. "Yep," he said. "Just like the old man."

· 16

Slocum held the whiskey glass to his lips and sipped delicately, savoring the flavor, but then he couldn't control himself. He swallowed the rest of the shot whole. His eyes began to water even before he could put the glass down. He smiled at Rachel Anderson across the table.

"It's a damn shame," he said. "If Paulson is kind enough to give us a bottle of the best bonded whiskey in New Mexico, you'd think the least I could do would be to taste it."

"You didn't do much better with your lunch," Rachel said, glancing at the empty plate by Slocum's glass.

The food on her own plate remained untouched, the grilled steak and the potatoes getting cold while Rachel stabbed at them listlessly with her fork. Nor was her heart in the conversation. She hadn't said more than a dozen words since her father and Henry Wingfield disappeared into the desert.

She had given up arguing with them early on, understanding that it was useless. The little office had then emptied itself completely, five men and a beautiful redhaired woman filing out through the saloon to create a mild stir in the noon crowd. Paulson proclaimed to the bartender that Rachel and Slocum and Sheriff Wingfield and Foley Anderson were all entitled to the best food and drink available, on the house. But he never quite

177

managed to look any of them in the eye as the little
crowd moved outside, where everyone stood around in
front of the saloon as if they didn't know what to do
next.

Paulson had coughed and said he might as well get
over to the bank.

Kevin Anderson followed a few steps behind, hesitantly, until Paulson turned back to give him a hard
stare. When Kevin stopped, Paulson turned around and
kept going. Kevin looked back at the others, then, and
saw nothing in their eyes that encouraged him to stay.
He looked once more at the retreating saloon owner, and
finally moved off in the opposite direction with his head
hanging. A minute later he disappeared around a corner.

There had been another strained silence after that,
until Anderson and Wingfield renewed their excitement
over the idea of raiding Stonetown. Rachel and Slocum
followed them to the sheriff's office, where the two
men loaded up with rifles and extra ammunition, then
stood and watched them riding away. They continued
watching the horizon for a long time after the two riders
disappeared, and then they had decided to return to the
saloon before they rode out to the Lazy K.

Slocum wasn't sure exactly what was troubling the
woman. The list of possibilities was sure long enough,
but it didn't seem that she was grieving so much as it
seemed that she was wrestling with something.

"How will it feel to be the boss?" he finally asked.

"It's a hell of a price to pay, Slocum. I'd rather have
my father."

"You've had him for a long time so far," Slocum
suggested. "And when you think about it, who can
really tell how much longer—"

Rachel's eyes stopped him. "Don't," she said. "You
know as well as I do he's not coming back. Don't treat
me like a child."

"Fair enough," Slocum said evenly. "I expect you're

right. He's probably hoping to stop a bullet out there so he doesn't have to come back to wait out his time. You don't think that's right?"

Rachel was resting her chin against the palm of her hand, watching her other hand poke a fork at a piece of potato.

"I guess you'd rather he come back to be with you," Slocum said. "Even if it means he spends his days in pain and the nights waiting—"

"I get your point, Slocum! I'm being selfish. I *know* that, I guess. It's just . . ." She exhaled sharply, glancing at the sun pouring through the door. "I don't know, it just seems so unfair."

Slocum studied her for a moment, and then spoke more gently. "I know," he said. "Or I think I do. All those years he never gave you a chance. And now that he *believes* in you . . . well, he won't be around for you to show him what you can really do."

Rachel blinked several times, tears brimming over and flowing freely.

"You were close to him when you were a little girl, weren't you?" Slocum said. "Then you were close to him again for just a few minutes, in the office, and you wish it could have lasted longer."

"A *lot* longer," Rachel said, still staring at the plate, her chin in the palm of her hand. "That's part of it, I guess. But it's Kevin, too. I feel like I just . . . climbed right over him, somehow."

"Oh, Lord!" Slocum said. "You're feeling guilty about Kevin?"

She nodded, not looking up. "Didn't you see the way he went slinking off? Like he doesn't have a friend left in the world?"

"He doesn't deserve one, Rachel. You can't blame— He did this to himself, don't you see that?"

"That's what I keep telling myself. But if I hadn't taken you back out to look for the herd . . ."

"Then Kevin probably would have gotten away with everything. Do you think he should have?"

"My father would be a lot happier."

"No!" Slocum said, so harshly that Rachel finally looked up at him. "For one thing, your father as much as said he suspected Kevin all along. At the very least, he knew Kevin wasn't fit to run the ranch. But he wouldn't admit it to himself, Rachel. All he could see was the whole tradition—the way things are supposed to be passed on from fathers to sons—and it was making him miserable to be doing something he knew wasn't right. No wonder he was hanging on."

Rachel was listening intently, and Slocum hoped that he was mostly telling the truth.

"But now he's seen what you can do, Rachel—he's heard those wonderful stories—and he knows he can trust you with the Lazy K. So he's free to go off on this last adventure with his oldest friend. Did you see them when they were riding out? Did you really see them, Rachel? I guarantee you that your father is happier at this moment—right *now,* feeling more *alive*—than he's been in years."

The corners of Rachel's mouth twitched suddenly, and then she was offering him a weak smile. "That's the finest line of horseshit I've ever heard in my life," she said, sighing deeply. "But maybe there's a little bit of truth in there. I hope so. I only wish—"

Her head snapped up suddenly and her eyes went wide. She started to yell something but Slocum was already twisting in his chair, trying to get out of a crouch with Kevin Anderson running at him from the black-curtained doorway. Several impressions seemed to hit Slocum at once, at about the same time that he was being bowled over by Anderson's wild rush. He was thinking that Kevin must have come through the back door of the building. He was also thinking that Kevin's face was distorted with madness. *The man is crazy,* he thought. *He's dangerous*. Kevin Anderson was on top of Slocum and Slocum couldn't move. The big man weighed him down. Slocum was frantically twisting and turning, trying to get leverage, energized by terror, but it was hopeless. Kevin's big knees were pinning Slocum's shoulders while the man's massive fists pounded his face. He felt his cheeks splitting open and the back of his head slamming into the wooden floor. Someone was screaming but the voice seemed to be getting farther and farther away. Slocum kept thinking, *I've got to stop this or he'll kill me*. But he couldn't move his arms, and the voice was still getting farther away.

Then he felt a curious sensation, followed by a shudder, and a moment later the great weight on his chest and shoulders was falling away. He was having trouble seeing things at first, but slowly he became aware of a body lying next to him. He squeezed his eyes closed and then looked again. The body was Kevin—the man who'd attacked him.

There was another body standing above him. Slocum looked up and realized it was the bartender, with a long chunk of wood hanging by his side.

"Thanks," Slocum said hoarsely. "That was even better than the whiskey."

Slocum worked himself onto his hands and knees, then decided to rest there for a minute, aware of the blood running off his face and onto the floor. Rachel Anderson had come to stand over him, next to the bartender.

"As far as Kevin goes," said Slocum, as if continuing their conversation after a minor interruption. "Offhand, I'd say he blames me more for what happened than he blames you."

Slocum put his Colt on the table while he finished off the bottle of whiskey, for medicinal purposes. Rachel was off getting their horses from the livery stable.

Kevin woke up after a few minutes, raising his big head to see Slocum pointing the Colt at his chest. The two men measured each other with cold looks, until Slocum decided to cock the revolver for added effect. Kevin picked up his hat then and stood up, pausing to stare at Slocum once again.

"This ain't over," he said.

"That's fine with me," said Slocum. "I'll be keeping an eye on my back, which is where I'm likely to see you again."

"Damn right!" Kevin said, as if he hadn't understood the insult. "But you won't see me because you'll be dead. You're a dead man already, only you don't know it yet."

It was a pretty accurate description of the way Slocum felt. The ride to the Lazy K seemed to take forever, and once he got there he couldn't seem to do anything but sleep for a few days. It began to worry him, making him wonder if his need for sleep meant that there might be permanent damage from all the beating his head had been taking.

Mitch Boyd teased him at first—before he started giving Slocum darkly suspicious looks—accusing him of faking his injuries so he could stay in the house with Rachel while the segundo and his vaqueros had to go to work each day.

Slocum was forced to admit he was finally enjoying the soft bed, which he'd been promised on his first night there, and also the attention of not one but two women. Rachel and Julie had hit it off, once they had a chance to talk, and Julie had been allowed to stay for a while. The little blonde seemed to be indifferent to the rest of the workers—she told Slocum she didn't want to bother much with men—but she wouldn't leave him alone. She even slipped into bed with him a couple of times, when Rachel had gone out to check a water hole or find a horse. But she spent most of her time talking about

Rachel, saying she wanted to be just like her, and she had never known a woman could be like that.

"Like what?" Slocum had asked.

"You know. Making decisions and all . . . telling people what to do. I bet no one ever beats her."

Slocum was up and around by the fourth day, sitting in the shade in front of the ranch house, when Henry Wingfield rode up. The sheriff was leading Foley Anderson's horse with a bundle draped over the saddle. Slocum stood to meet him, noticing that Rachel was coming up from the barn with Julie at her side. The sheriff stopped his horse in front of Slocum and handed down a black hat with a band of silver conchos around the crown.

"Foley said this was yours," Wingfield said gravely. "He told me to tell you it was the least he could do."

Slocum took the hat and turned it over in his hands, not trusting himself to speak, feeling relieved when the sheriff turned his attention to the approaching women.

"Stonetown is gone," Wingfield told Rachel. "We burned everything we could, and what outlaws we didn't kill, we chased clear into Mexico." The old man began to falter. "Maybe we paid a high price, Rachel, but . . ."

"I understand," the woman said calmly, glancing at the tarpaulin-covered bundle on her father's horse. "Not many of us get to choose how we leave this world, do we, Sheriff?"

"No, ma'am," said Wingfield. He climbed stiffly down from his horse.

Rachel was contemplating her father's body again while the sheriff looked at her with a fatherly expression and Julie watched her with open admiration. *Here was a woman who would never be defeated,* she seemed to be thinking. *I wonder if I could learn . . .*

"I figure the story will be in the *Democrat* by Saturday," Wingfield said. "And for what it's worth, Rachel, when I get done tellin' the story your father will be a legend hereabouts."

The woman looked at the sheriff with a soft smile. "I suppose a legend's as good a thing to leave behind as any," she said. "But don't sell your part of the story short."

The sheriff smiled too, for the first time. "I won't have to," he said. "But I mean it, Rachel. People will be talking about Foley Anderson as long as there's people in New Mexico to talk."

"Thank you, Mr. Wingfield. I wonder if I could ask another favor of you."

"Anything."

"Find my brother and tell him what's happened. Tell him I'll meet with him so we can talk out how to handle the ranch."

"But your father—"

"I know what he said, Sheriff, but I'm sure his will leaves the Lazy K to my brother. So, to be strictly legal . . ."

Her voice trailed off as Wingfield walked around to the other side of his horse and began rummaging through his saddlebags. "You didn't let me finish," he said. "Foley thought of that the first night out, Rachel. He wrote up a new document and had me sign it as a witness so I could file it with his lawyer. The only time it mentions Kevin, it says he's already been taken care of. You are now the sole owner of the Lazy K."

Rachel closed her eyes and began swaying a little. Slocum moved closer so he could catch her if he had to. Wingfield was still digging.

"Here it is," he said suddenly, pulling out a ragged piece of brown paper that had been folded over once.

"That's all right," said the woman, "I don't need to see it."

"This is something else he wrote. He wanted me to give it to you."

Rachel accepted it with trembling fingers, staring at it as if she was afraid to open it. Wingfield looked across her and caught Slocum's eye, motioning with his head toward Anderson's horse. Together the two men unloaded the rancher's body and carried it toward the house while Julie led the horse toward the barn, leaving Rachel alone with her message.

Wingfield led them automatically to the room Slocum had been using, a kind of parlor, but he stopped in the doorway when he noticed Slocum's gear.

"That's all right," Slocum told him. "I'll be on my way this afternoon."

Wingfield looked startled. "You can't leave her today!" he said, shifting the weight of his dead friend in his arms. "She'll need someone now more than ever."

"I know, Sheriff. But I don't want it to be me."

The old man's expression was darkening into anger.

"She's already got someone," Slocum hurried to explain, nudging ahead slightly so that Wingfield remembered to help him carry Anderson's body the rest of the way to the bed. "She's got a good man who wants to stick by her the rest of her life."

"You mean Boyd?" said Wingfield.

Slocum nodded. *"He's* the one I want her to turn to, when she's ready."

There was a musty gleam in the sheriff's eye. "Nice footwork," he said. "But why don't you go see her for now—see how she's doing—and let me have a little more time with my friend."

Rachel hadn't moved. Slocum stood in the doorway and watched her for a while, but all she did was gaze at the piece of brown paper. Finally he stepped out beneath the ramada, tentatively, ready to retreat if she seemed to resent his presence.

Instead she held out the piece of paper, taking hold of his arm and squeezing it against her body when he began to study the rough scrawl of her father's hand.

There wasn't much to read.

"I hope you can forgive an old man his blindness," the note said. "I only thank the Lord my eyes were opened in time. You stand as living proof that I managed to do at least one thing right."

JAKE LOGAN

___	07139-1	SOUTH OF THE BORDER	$2.50
___	07567-2	SLOCUM'S PRIDE	$2.50
___	07382-3	SLOCUM AND THE GUN-RUNNERS	$2.50
___	07494-3	SLOCUM'S WINNING HAND	$2.50
___	08382-9	SLOCUM IN DEADWOOD	$2.50
___	07973-2	SLOCUM AND THE AVENGING GUN	$2.50
___	08087-0	THE SUNSHINE BASIN WAR	$2.50
___	08279-2	VIGILANTE JUSTICE	$2.50
___	08189-3	JAILBREAK MOON	$2.50
___	08392-6	SIX GUN BRIDE	$2.50
___	08076-5	MESCALERO DAWN	$2.50
___	08539-6	DENVER GOLD	$2.50
___	08644-X	SLOCUM AND THE BOZEMAN TRAIL	$2.50
___	08742-5	SLOCUM AND THE HORSE THIEVES	$2.50
___	08773-5	SLOCUM AND THE NOOSE OF HELL	$2.50
___	08791-3	CHEYENNE BLOODBATH	$2.50
___	09088-4	THE BLACKMAIL EXPRESS	$2.50
___	09111-2	SLOCUM AND THE SILVER RANCH FIGHT	$2.50
___	09299-2	SLOCUM AND THE LONG WAGON TRAIN	$2.50

Available at your local bookstore or return this form to

 BERKLEY
THE BERKLEY PUBLISHING GROUP, Dept. B
390 Murray Hill Parkway, East Rutherford, NJ 07073

Please send me the titles checked above. I enclose _____ Include $1.00 for postage
and handling if one book is ordered, add 25¢ per book for two or more not to exceed
$1.75. California, Illinois, New Jersey and Tennessee residents please add sales tax
Prices subject to change without notice and may be higher in Canada

NAME_____

ADDRESS_____

CITY _____ STATE/ZIP _____

(Allow six weeks for delivery)

162b

GREAT WESTERN YARNS FROM ONE OF THE BEST-SELLING WRITERS IN THE FIELD TODAY

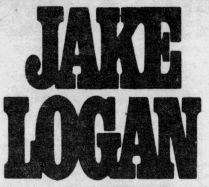

JAKE LOGAN

___	0-867-21003	**BLOODY TRAIL TO TEXAS**	$1.95
___	0-867-21041	**THE COMANCHE'S WOMAN**	$1.95
___	0-872-16979	**OUTLAW BLOOD**	$1.95
___	06191-4	**THE CANYON BUNCH**	$2.25
___	06255-4	**SLOCUM'S JUSTICE**	$2.25
___	05958-8	**SLOCUM'S RAID**	$1.95
___	0-872-16823	**SLOCUM'S CODE**	$1.95
___	0-867-21071	**SLOCUM'S DEBT**	$1.95
___	0-867-21090	**SLOCUM'S GOLD**	$1.95
___	0-867-21023	**SLOCUM'S HELL**	$1.95
___	0-867-21087	**SLOCUM'S REVENGE**	$1.95
___	07665-2	**SLOCUM GETS EVEN**	$2.75
___	06744-0	**SLOCUM AND THE LOST DUTCHMAN MINE**	$2.50
___	06846-3	**GUNS OF THE SOUTH PASS**	$2.50
___	07258-4	**DALLAS MADAM**	$2.50